Joseph Cox's

Medicine

And other Torah Stories

Volume 1:
Genesis - בראשית

Joseph J. Cox

Published by Big Picture Books

Modiin, Israel

Cover Photography by Prince Akachi on Unsplash

Edited by Wouter Dreyer

Feedback from many friends & associates – you know who you are!

Dedicated to G-d,
May my work be blessing for the Almighty

Contents

Introduction

The idea of using stories to explain moral concepts is probably as old as human vocabulary itself. Stories, not rules or arguments, have generational impact, transferring values from one generation to the next. They establish and explain the core character of the societies that carry them. Because of this power, stories have long been used to explain concepts in the Torah.

However, to modern ears many such stories are foreign; either their concepts are unfamiliar, or their styles fail to grip the modern conscious.

This book provides a new set of modern, relatable and engaging stories. They cross many genres and are meant to engage many different kinds of people. I know that writing them has left me with a far stronger understanding of the Torah, of humanity and of the world that surrounds us.

Perhaps you, the reader, can find that same understanding. And, perhaps, these stories will also strengthen your relationship to G-d and your understanding of our place in the world.

Thank you,

Joseph Cox

Book of Bereshit: Joseph Sato

The shocks powers its way through my body. The music, filling the club with its throbbing, excited beat, seems to pull away from *my* reality. It is replaced by a simple, stunned, fear.

I look at my phone, the message from my best friend burning into my mind.

And then I look up and I see *him*, walking towards me – with two drinks in hand.

I don't know what to do. But I do know the next five minutes will decide the course of my life.

--

It had all started innocently enough. My dad had been pressuring me for weeks to go on a date with a guy from his work. I was *not* interested. My father was pretty much the last person I 'd think of as a source of romantic guidance.

While my parents were still married, their own relationship had been smashed to pieces. The story is too long to share here, but they stayed together for appearances. They are what you might call 'public figures.' I won't go into names, but as prominent politicians, being seen as being in a strong marriage is like being seen to have principles; it can be critical to the possibility of career advancement.

I didn't want to follow in their path.

I was happy with my relationships, and I didn't need a job. Sure, the relationships didn't last long. But they didn't need to. Variety is the spice of life, right? I had everything I needed. Money, beauty, even a great sense of adventure and endless possibilities for satisfying it.

None of that gelled with going on a date suggested by my politically oriented father. I was far happier being their wayward and somewhat off-color daughter.

Then a few weeks into his light pestering my father showed me a picture of the guy. I can describe him in one word. *Gorgeous.* He was just a beautiful man. He was Japanese and somehow seemed strong and soft and welcoming and protecting all at once. I hemmed and hawed. I had to. I didn't want taking parental advice to risk turning into a pattern. But then I agreed. My dad was grinning about his victory. He promised to set something up.

I had expected the guy to be in DC, that's where both my father and I both lived. What I got was an address in *Manhattan*.

I thought about skipping the whole thing then and there, but he *was a beautiful man*. So, I decided to go. Naturally, I took the train. That's one thing I do for my father. I always ride Amtrak when I can – it makes him look good with his political base. New York is freezing cold and blanketed in snow, but the train somehow still runs on time – generally.

Soon enough, thanks to a brave cabbie who slid his way up Broadway, I found myself outside an Upper West Side restaurant called the Bactria Grill. The name itself almost seemed like a health code violation.

But I'd come all this way. So, I opened the door and was suddenly hit with a wave of deep and intense smells. Intense smells and darkness. There was a small cubicle there, a greeting area. And there was a man there, waiting for me. He was a little rough looking, but he seemed to be expecting me.

In an accent I couldn't place, he offered to take my coat, which I gave him. And then he asked me to take off my shoes, which I did. And then he ushered me beyond the cubicle and into the main dining room.

I saw the room first. It was unlike any restaurant I'd ever been in before. There were massive, intricately decorated curtains hanging from the ceiling along with dim lights in dark carved metal lanterns. There were *carpets* on the floors. The effect was almost magical.

The room was empty except for one area right in the middle. There wasn't a table there though. Instead, there was a square woven cloth spread over the floor with glasses and a pitcher of water in the center of it. Sitting cross-legged on one corner was the man, the man from the photograph.

He lifted his eyes, saw me, and fluidly rose from the floor to greet me. With a flourish of his hand, he waved me to the carpet.

He was just as gorgeous as his photo had suggested.

I walked over and with a slight bow he said, in another accent I couldn't place, "I'm Joseph Sato."

"Charlotte," I answered. I felt almost like sticking my hand out for him to shake, or kiss. But for some reason I knew that wasn't the right thing to do.

He gestured towards a spot opposite him. And I sat there, cross-legged, sinking to the floor as gracefully as I could manage. Were we really going to eat on the floor? And where was everybody else?

A waiter hovered nearby.

I don't know what drove my decision, but I decided to go with humor.

"Well," I said, "I just dragged myself up from D.C. to meet you. Is it going to be worth it?"

I sounded a touch more aggressive than I felt. But the kind of men I like tend to appreciate that.

Joseph's face remained entirely serious. In a steady voice he said, "I can't guarantee *I'll* be worth it. But the *food* is fantastic."

I looked around a little doubtfully. After all, who puts carpets on a restaurant floor? Talk about Bactria.

"Let me order?" he said. It is a question, but also a suggestion and perhaps a foregone conclusion.

I nodded and waved my hand to grant my permission. He smiled at that and then tipped his head up to the hovering waiter and let out a stream of some magical mellifluous sounding words. The waiter answered with a brief burst of his own and then turned away from us.

I wasn't going to let him get me to ask what language he was speaking. I don't like to appear impressed – much less fawning. Instead, I asked, "What'd you order?"

"Kabuli Palaw," he answered.

I nodded, pretending to know what the heck he was talking about.

We sank back into silence. After what seemed like a significant period of discomfort, he leaned forward and poured a bit of water for me and then for himself. We each lifted up our glasses to drink.

"Why here?" I asked.

He smiles. "Simple," he said, "This is the best Afghani restaurant on the eastern seaboard."

"You enjoy the exotic?" I asked.

"No, not really," he answered, "I grew up in Afghanistan."

I wasn't certain what kind of response he was expecting, but I came to a quick conclusion. "Which NGO did your parents work for?"

"None," he said, "My family has been in rural Afghanistan for 4 generations."

That I didn't expect.

I was about to ask a follow-up question when our food appeared. It was delivered on a single massive plate piled high with the most aromatic rice I'd ever imagined. I watched, hungrily, as the waiter placed the plate between us.

I looked at the rice and I picked out the flavors with my eyes. There were raisins, carrots, orange peels, baked almonds and, yes, succulent meat mixed in with the golden grains of the rice itself.

"Kabuli Palaw?" I asked.

"Kabuli Palaw," said Joseph Sato, with another polite nod.

I looked around, wondering where *my* plate was. That was when a second waiter appeared. But instead of bearing plates, he had a large bowl and a small pitcher. He crouched next to Joseph and ran the water over his right hand. He then turned to me, and I extended my right hand which was also washed.

"Plates?" I asked. But Joseph just smiled and extended his right hand towards the food. He took a collection of the rice in his fingers, gathering is into a little ball. And then he brought it back to his mouth. His eyes closed as he took his first bite, and he smiled in obvious pleasure and joy.

It was all remarkably sophisticated; considering he was eating with his fingers.

I mimicked him, reaching towards the food. When I tasted it, I understood the pleasure. The rice was incredible.

"The food is worth it," I said.

"Yes," he said, "It is."

"So, what brought your family to Afghanistan?"

"My great-grandparents," he answered, between morsels of rice. "My great-grandfather actually. He had this idea, before World War I, when Japan was just starting to get seriously militaristic, that the future lay in the middle."

"The middle?"

"Yes," he said, "He believed it lay in the space between civilizations. Between East and West, between Christian and Muslim and Hindu, between all the great powers. And so, he moved to Afghanistan."

"A Muslim country?"

"Certainly," said Sato, "But one that had been many other things as well. It has long been a crossroads. This place is named after ancient Bactria, which was a legendary Greek trading empire. When my father moved there it was independent, kind of. But Britain controlled its foreign policy. As he saw it, a true mix."

I tasted some more of the food. Joseph asked the waiter for something else. A moment later, there was a flask of Sake. It seemed a little incongruous.

"But why?"

"He believed he and his children could be a blessing to the rest of mankind; by being in the middle of it. They could understand others better, perhaps. I don't really know. I don't think he did either."

"Did you live in Kabul?"

"No, we lived in a fortress of our own. It was almost like my great-grandfather was a warlord. But he didn't really have his own clan, which made it hard."

I could imagine.

"How'd he survive?"

8

"Not easily. He just managed to make unsteady alliances. Japan is an honor-focused society, and so is Afghanistan. But they aren't quite the same. One time my great-grandfather married a local, in order to forge an alliance. But my great-grandmother was something of a battle axe and she wouldn't let the woman's children be counted as part of the family. The whole affair almost got them all killed. My grandfather, my great-grandfather's son, was kidnapped at once point, and almost killed. But, somehow, he made it."

I nodded, still uncertain why he'd take that kind of risk with his family.

"I respect him," said Sato, "He took a terrible risk, but he opened us up to a new reality. I wouldn't be the same person if he hadn't."

I nodded again, not quite getting it. And then I asked, "Are there normally tables here?"

"Yes," said Joseph, with a sheepish grin, "I asked them to be taken away. There are also plates and forks and spoons and knives. I wanted you to have the full experience."

We kept eating. We talked about my family. He seemed to know an enormous amount about it and about me. But, still, he listened to what *I* had to say. He hadn't reached any conclusions. He was almost disconcertingly interested in me.

Eventually, we wrapped up dinner. We rose from the floor and as we moved towards the front, a phalanx of waitstaff appeared. In moments, it seemed, our unique little setting was removed, and all the normal accouterments of a Manhattan restaurant appeared. Joseph helped me with my coat, somehow managing not to touch me as he did so. And then we stepped outside. There was a line outside the restaurant.

I realized, in a moment of shame, that all these people had been waiting for us to leave.

A car pulled up to the curb, a massive Mercedes limousine. A driver emerged and opened the curbside door. I folded myself in and Joseph followed. The car was warm and welcoming and extremely comfortable. There were crystal wine glasses, a decanter and all the fixings of top-tier luxury.

"What about your grandfather, after he was kidnapped?"

"He was always scared after that," said Joseph, "He always wanted to hold on to what he could feel. He really didn't agree with what his father had done. But he also couldn't go back to Japan. He'd be a foreigner; he wouldn't know how to live. And so, he stayed, even though it was hard. He became quite a rich man, actually. But that was his entire focus. The only thing that saved him was his wife."

"You don't look even a little Afghani," I said, "Was she?"

"No," said Joseph, "His wife was also Japanese."

"How'd he find her in Afghanistan?"

"She just showed up. She somehow had the same idea as my great-grandfather. She wanted to do something for humanity and somehow, she figured it started with settling in rural Afghanistan. She heard about us and even before she showed up, she decided she was going to marry my grandfather – the second generation of our Japanese family in Afghanistan. He became her project."

I was about to ask a question, but the car pulled over. "Ice cream?" asked Sato.

"In winter?" I asked.

"It isn't that cold."

I glanced sideways at him, not quite believing what he'd said.

"I'll get it," he offered. With that, he pulled open the door and stepped outside. There was an ice cream place, really just a hole in the wall. And there was a line. A small line of shivering people lining up to get a freezing cold dessert. I saw Sato there. He *looked* cold, no matter what he said.

I pulled my phone from my pocket. My most trusted friend was a Secret Service agent who'd been assigned to me when I'd been younger. I texted her one question, "Joseph Sato, is he for real?"

And then I looked out the window and realized that I desperately wanted to be with Sato. With that, I opened the door, stepped out of the car and joined him in line.

"I assume she succeeded?" I asked.

"Who?" he said.

"Your grandmother, at marrying your grandfather?"

"Ah, yes," he said, "Eventually, she did. My grandfather hoarded his money. He was constantly trying to protect it, not least from the people he hired to protect him and his family. His success was almost embarrassing to the other families in the area. They grew pretty jealous. But all he saw was the money and the walls giving him the feeling of safety he so badly craved."

"Did it keep him safe?"

"Yes. But it was an empty life, and she knew it. When he was already an old man my grandmother tricked him into funding a little school in the area. He was angry about it, at first. But then, when a few of the local boys signed up, he began to visit. He began to watch them and even help out with the teaching. And he began to respect his own father. That's how I heard it anyway. His resentment at being in that place changed to appreciation for it; like he suddenly realized there was something truly worthwhile there. And that something was in the people, not the wealth."

I could see clearly that Sato respected what his grandfather had learned.

We got to the window and ordered. Moments later we had our ice cream. When I turned around, the car was no longer there. When I glanced at Sato, he seemed unperturbed. Instead, he smiled at me and said, "The ice cream will last longer this way."

He took a lick, and I followed suit. My head was freezing, but I had it anyway. I was interested in this man, interested enough to have ice cream (albeit delicious ice cream) on a freezing winter night.

We walked down the street, side by side. Eventually, our ice creams consumed, we came to a club. Loud, throbbing, music was pouring out of the door.

A bouncer saw Joseph, nodded at him, spoke his name and ushered us inside.

The stop was far from unplanned. The man had certainly put a great deal of thought into this date. I wondered where he'd like it to end up. I'd have been happy with anything he'd have been happy with.

"What about your father?" I asked, trying to project over the sound of the club.

I felt my phone vibrate, but I ignored it. We headed to the bar and Joseph grabbed a couple of screwdrivers that are already waiting for us. They are my favorite.

We made our way to a small table along the edge of the room.

"My father joined the Communists," Sato continued, at a near shout, "He was upset about everything. Despite all his blessings he wasn't satisfied. He wanted to rebuild everything the way he wanted it and he wanted to do it then and there. And for a little while it looked like it would work. The Soviets invaded and he aligned himself with them. But Afghan culture wasn't going to be reinvented in a day. He dishonored those around him, and *everybody* turned on him. He fled to Kabul. But once the Communists were driven out, he wasn't safe there either. My grandfather ended up sending him away, back to distant relatives in Japan."

"But you grew up in Afghanistan."

"Yes, but I was born in Japan."

"Did your father stay a Communist?"

"No, the man I knew growing up was a master of self-control. I think he realized he was totally dependent on his Japanese family. His wife helped him realize that he had to respect family and tradition. He had to change things slowly, not burn them down. Any other path was doomed to failure. He married in Japan and then he ended up moving back to Afghanistan. I guess I learned from him too. You've got to take things slowly."

I nodded, clinking my glass to his and tipping back my drink.

That's what I'd do, I realized. I'd take things slowly. Here, with Sato. They'd last longer that way.

"What about you?" I asked, "Why are you here?"

"I'm here to manage a research effort."

"Really?" I asked.

"Yes," he said, "Central Asia is a bit of a hotbed for phage research."

"Phage?" I wasn't certain I'd heard him correctly over the noise of the place.

"They are viruses that fight bacteria. As antibiotics get less and less effective people are beginning to look at using phages for solutions. I'm an expert and so that's what I'm doing. I'm leading an international effort to save the world."

He said the last bit with a bit of a chuckle; but I realized he was entirely serious.

I was a bit blown away by that. In that moment, for the first time in my life, I almost felt outclassed by *a guy*.

"Another drink?" Sato asked.

"Just a Coke," I said. He smiled again, then got up from our little table and headed back towards the bar.

I watched him go and realized, with surprise, that I could spend the rest of my life with this man.

In that instant, I remembered my earlier question. Was he for real? I almost didn't want to know. Nonetheless, I grabbed my phone from my pocket.

My friend, the Secret Service agent, had texted me back.

The shock of her message powers its way through my body. The music, filling the club with its throbbing, excited beat, seems to pull away from *my* reality. It is replaced by a simple, stunned, fear.

I look at my phone, the message burning into my mind.

"He is rich. He is successful. He is Afghani. And he *is a convicted rapist!*"

And then I look up and I see *him*, walking towards me – with two drinks in hand.

What do they have in them?

A chill runs through me as he approaches.

He puts the drinks on the little table. But I don't take mine. Should I just run?

"What about you?" I ask in as light a way as I can manage.

14

Sato smiles, but now it seems creepy. "I was my father's favorite and I thought I'd just get everything he had. I was greedy. I dishonored those around me. I ended up leaving just like my father did. But I came here, not to Japan."

I push a bit more, "You're what in your mid-thirties? Why haven't you been snatched up already?"

He pauses for a moment, considers, and then says, "My great-grandfather's mission was to change the world by connecting with people. Not through wealth or isolation or revolution. I can't live up to that mission. I drive those around me crazy. I care far more about ideas than I do about people. And so, I need someone who balances me. I need someone who can care about people. I need someone to carry on my grandfather's vision. I might be trying to save the world, but there had to be something I'm saving it for."

I find myself twisted inside. It all sounds so beautiful, so elevated. So hopeful. So, flattering. But he's a rapist and he's just spun me a line.

He continues, though, "I haven't found anybody. But I also haven't been looking for very long."

"Why not?" I ask, "Your work was all-consuming?"

"No," he says, "I haven't been looking because when I was 20 years-old I was convicted of rape and sentenced to life in prison."

I just stare at him.

"Did you do it?" I ask, in a near whisper. I don't know how he can hear me over the music, but he seems to.

"No," he says, "In those days I made a lot of people angry. I thought I was the best in the world. The best in my family. I found fault with everybody who came before me and everybody who knew me. A lot of people were impressed, for a while. But then they started to hate me. Eventually, I pissed off the wrong person, put myself in a compromising situation and I found myself in prison"

I don't know whether to believe him.

"Why are you out?" I ask.

"Phages," he says, "They knew I was an expert in phages. There are new strains of bacteria out there that are scaring the heck out of people. So, they pulled me out and gave me a little presentation about one particular bacterial agent. I watched it and I understood the mistakes they had made which had led to this superbug. I was going to criticize them for it. But in that moment, I understood another truth. In that moment I realized that I could see the faults of the people who came before me: My great-grandfather's crazy faith, my grandfather's materialism, my father's destructiveness. Or I could honor them for what they learned and what they'd become. As I sat there across from those frightened scientists, I realized I could honor my ancestors for what they'd learned. I showed them how I could help them. I showed them how *they* could save the world. I showed them the credit they would be due. And the President himself granted me a reprieve."

"A pardon?"

"No, just a reprieve. Off-the-books in a way. My conviction was never overturned." I stare at him, almost stunned in my confusion. What do I do?

Do I believe that he is not a rapist? Do I believe that he has changed? Or is it all a setup more fictional than anything my own parents had even concocted.

The safe path is to run. But I've never met anybody like this. I've never met anybody who has made me feel like *I* could change the world.

I replay the date in my mind and suddenly it all starts to click into place.

He had brought me to the restaurant, without forks and knives or plates, to see whether I could follow in his great-grandfather's footsteps and embrace the foreign.

He had brought me to the ice cream place to see whether I could walk in the footsteps of his grandfather and step out into the cold, putting relationships over material comfort.

He had brought me to the club to see whether I would take things slow, having only the one drink and letting reality unfold bit by bit.

And now this. He's testing whether I will give him credit for who is and what he has learned, rather than who he had been.

I look at him, realizing that my life hinges on this moment – this decision.

And then I pick up the Coke and drink the entire thing.

This story is based on the family arc in Bereshit (Genesis). Avraham (Abraham) is the man who settles in the lands between the Fertile Crescent and Egypt. His father was the first person in the Torah to move *between* civilizations. He has a crazy faith that *somehow* he will be a blessing to the families of the world. Sarah protects his legacy – realizing that a life of giving would not, by itself, create a sustainable reality.

Yitzchak (Isaac) was almost killed for his father's faith. He embraces the physical, 'playing' with his wife and becoming the only one of the forefathers to farm and loving his son Esav (Esau) because of Esav's physicality. Eventually, he learns to embraces Yaacov (Jacob) and blesses him with his own father's relationship to G-d.

Yaacov is a revolutionary, angry about his place in the world. He destroys all the conventions around him. But then he flees back to his own grandfather's homeland and learns to move slowly – with self-control.

And Yosef (Joseph) is conceited. He is banished by his brothers and then imprisoned for a rape he didn't commit. He is freed when he gives credit to G-d and then recognizes Pharaoh's potential to rescue the land itself.

Shortly afterwards, he is married to Asnat.

While we don't learn much about Charlotte in this story, she is Asnat. Her husband is always travelling, rescuing Egypt. She raises their children, the first sons in the Torah who don't fight because they are motivated by a greater vision. And Asnat is the only wife mentioned in the lists of Yaacov's family who came down to Egypt. She alone, among the wives of Yaacov's sons, is counted as a part of Yaacov's family.

Asnat married a man convicted of rape and jailed for a number of years.

She may or may not have chosen her groom, but she grew through him and balanced his great weaknesses.

Some part of the story of Avraham's family is about finding the best in people, honoring that and learning from it. Ultimately it is about raising humanity by recognizing the best of what humanity can be.

As we pass from generation to generation, we build upon the past instead of being trapped in it.

Our forefathers showed us the way. By learning from them not only as individuals, but as children learning from the lives of their parents, we can all ultimately be raised up.

Bereshit: The Gnome

They call me the gnome. They've always called me the gnome. I didn't use to care. I never used to care what other people thought of me. I hardly gave consideration to what I thought of myself. I just am. Others can worry about currying the favor and praise of their peers. That has never been my concern. I've always acted as *I* felt was right.

And yet, right now, I care. I'm writing this letter, this explanation, because I care.

I'm on the verge of destroying my life's work, because I care.

But before I do, I must submit myself to your judgment. I submit myself because I do not know what is right.

I grew up in the Palestinian town of Bayt Sira. It is a tiny town; only a few thousand people live there. The terrain is rough and uneven. Bayt Sira literally means "the house of the fold." The land folds around us with our orange-domed mosque positioned at the top of a small hill. When I was a young boy, I would climb the hills around our little village and look down at the picture-perfect town. The beautiful mosque rose from the middle of it. And all around, scattered like dice thrown by All-h Himself, were the houses we lived in.

Not many years before I was born, the Israelis established a city on the border of my town. You could make out their children playing in the yards of the villas they built. They were only 300 meters from the edges of our homes. But they were so different. They built in ordered lines, governed by some unseen hand. They reshaped the land to fit their plans. More often than not, *we* reshaped the land for them; the men in our town building their city. While we conformed to the logic of the hills and the needs of those who built each building, they seemed to be governed by some larger plan. Our newest buildings resemble theirs; we have copied their architecture. So much is different. We have never copied their planning, sure. But the very scent of our lives was different. Ours was a land almost barren of trees. The smell of the high desert; the faint odor of life's resistance to nature, pervaded our world. But, when the winds shifted, we could catch the odors of Maccabim. The tree-lined streets and beautiful homes were so close to us. But it was their scent, the scent of life, that cultivated our resentment.

We were not good neighbors. Even as we worked for the Israelis, earning our money building their city, we fought against it. The latest rumors, conspiracies and injustices would fly through our town just like any other town. And the young men and boys would protest. The Israelis eventually shut down the road that ran in the gap between our two towns. It was too risky to use.

After the protests, the boys would come back to the village, sharing stories of their exploits in the face of the occupiers. They would boast of their bravery in front of the girls. And they would mock me as I watched them. They mocked *everybody* who didn't take part. We were cowards. We were failing to stand up for our people. But I didn't react. I just watched. To me they all seemed like simple and empty toys. They were so predictable. I was not interested in them.

I suppose that's why I got into the models. These weren't the kinds of models you buy in a shop and assemble. No, I gathered scraps of this and that: bicycle chains, twigs, sticks and rocks. And I built models. I built tiny homes and tiny cars and tiny people. I built a miniature version of my village. Those who saw it could identify the tiny people who stood in its streets. There was Ibrahim, the mayor. There was Ahmed, who ran the grocery store. Children stood stock still in my little streets – frozen in play. But in my mind, the people in my village did things that *weren't* expected. It was engaging in that way. It was far more interesting than my reality.

I built a little Maccabim as well. I imagined what their people would look like. They were so close but aside from the occasional soldier, I never really saw them in person.

And soldiers, of course, don't look like people; they're not allowed to.

I spent all my time on the model. Eventually, it got too large for my parent's home. Luckily, one of the buildings on the edge of our village's central square was abandoned. It was made of a faded and crumbling orange concrete. It had a musty and dilapidated smell. Nobody wanted to live in it. The windows had been removed and repurposed for another home.

I moved my model there. I moved it and I kept building.

I didn't really live in Bayt Sira anymore. No, I lived in my imaginary village, spending all of my time within it. It grew more and more complex. People started to come to see it. One night, a group of boys crushed my miniature Maccabim and laid my little Jewish people down in puddles of ketchup. I didn't curse the boys who did it. They were just simple toys, repeating the actions they had been programmed for. They were mindless. But the Imam did curse them. He was fascinated by my work, and he protected it.

I rebuilt Maccabim, and they never crushed it again.

But even as I rebuilt it, I realized my two towns had no real movement. They had no real life. They were a replica of reality, and they were even more static than reality itself. The differences were only in my head. Only in my head did the people do the unexpected. And so, I began to play out a different reality with the model itself.

Houses moved locations. Roads began to take different paths. The fixed reality of the place began to change. The changes were subtle at first. But people noticed the changes. It drew more and more people. They would visit from Bayt Liqya and Safa and other nearby villages. They would watch my model and be sucked into it. They would ask questions about why things were the way they were.

But I had no time for them. Their reality was not of interest to me.

My model was developing, but it was still static. I wanted more of my imagination to come to life. And so, I learned about mechanical devices. I learned about springs and actuators and wheels and gears. And I started to make little cars that would drive on the roads. And I kept learning. And I managed to make little dogs and little people that would move through my village. The place was coming alive.

The visitors began to come from further and further away. They would watch my little wind-up people and then they would watch them move from place to place. They would watch them do things they would never do. They would watch them meet and seem to talk and interact in ways they would never interact. I liked to think it made them think. But I saw no evidence of that. The people remained predictable toys.

As I worked, the building around me was transformed. People were coming from Ramallah and Al-Quds and Bethlehem and Tulkarm to see my model. People were watching and asking and thinking. The village had repaired the building the model was in. They loved the tourism. The old musty smells disappeared. And the smell of my models, of old metal and oil cans and bits of wood, began to dominate the space.

But I was not satisfied. *My* mechanical people were no better than those cut-outs that surrounded me. They were no less predictable. I set them on their paths, and they followed them. I needed more. And so, I began to study artificial intelligence and biology and computing. And, bit by bit, I began to create a new kind of figurine for my model. One that could be rewarded and punished. One that could feel pleasure and pain.

I don't know exactly how, but I still remember the moment it came to life. And when it did, I realized that I wanted to *know* this little figurine. I wanted to relate to it. But how could it relate to me?

The answer was obvious. *I* built models and then watched them and interacted with them and imagined what might be. I wanted my little figurine to do the same. Then, we'd have something – a fundamental drive – in common.

I suppose I could have made the figurine make models. But then it would just have been another animatron. I wanted it to *live*. And so, I gave it a choice. It would receive a little joy from sitting around. But if it built and then rested, it would lose a little joy as it labored, but be granted a deeper and more fundamental joy in its time of rest. It would experience fulfillment. I gave it a choice, so that it *could* choose to know me.

But it did not create. It wandered, experiencing my little world. But it did not build like I built. And so, I placed my finger on the scales. I brought it pain. I brought it death. I made it so that it could only survive if it created like me. I forced it to be responsible for its choices.

And then, it did create. I was excited. I made dozens of the little thinking figurines. But then they stopped creating. They just stole, one from another. They stole what they needed and what they wanted. They overcame risk by taking from the others within the model.

I saw the pain and the loss, and the corruption and I wanted to destroy what I created.

And so, I did. I erased them all. All but one. And I began again. I gave them *law* this time. I taught *them* to kill so that theft and murder could be prevented. And their crimes subsided; corruption did not fill their world. But they did not reach out to *me*.

They only created what they needed. I could not relate to them. I thought about adding more pain, but I knew there would be no point. If I tipped the scales too much, they would once again be automatons.

I would be unable to relate to them.

My model was becoming more and more famous. Visitors were coming from other countries. Jews even came, under the protection of the Imam. Some even came from Maccabim. But the model was not safe. Some of those within my land considered it blasphemy. Others thought it an affront to our people and their pride. My figurines did not do as they would have done.

But I ignored them all. I lived in a different world.

I wanted to know the living things I had engendered. And then I realized the solution to my problem. I picked one of the little living figurines. And I added *more* pain and *more* joy to it. That one would lead. That one would be an example. Others would see it building and connecting with me and they would imitate it and find their way to me without coercion. They would see its joy, or they would see its pain. Either way, I would be able to relate.

The little figurine, the one I chose, cried out against the pain I caused it. It cried out against the horror and risk and death it encountered. But it did not walk in my path. It simply reached out

24

and begged. It did not understand what *I* wanted. It did not understand I wanted it to *know* me. Begging was not enough. Those around me knew how to beg All-h. I wanted it to walk in my path so I could truly relate to it. I wanted it to be better than the simple toys that surround me.

But it did not comply.

As time passed, I gave that singular figurine more and more pain. I laid incredible suffering upon it. But it did not learn. And I knew I must stop. I could not watch its cries of desperation to a creator who would not answer. The pain of it ate at my very soul.

I realized then, I realize now, that I could simply change that figurine. I could rob it of its free will. I could make it act as I want it to act. And then, perhaps, its peers will follow. But I also know that if I did that, I would be destroying it. I would be destroying the one I had chosen.

And ultimately, nothing will be learned or achieved.

And now? Now I do not know what to do.

Which is why I stand before you.

Because, for once, I do not know what to do.

Do I let the figurines just live and kill and destroy?

Do I force the chosen figurine, through pain or the removal of its will, to lead the others to a better future?

Do I force them to relate to me?

Or do I tear it all down, erasing the pain that fills the model I have created?

I do not know.

I am on the edge of destruction, and I do not know what I must do.

Perhaps, just maybe, that singular figurine will understand what I need of it.

Perhaps, just maybe, it will raise its head and understand its purpose, and all can be spared.

Or, perhaps not.

I do not know what to do.

G-d creates the world and then rests on Shabbat, making it Holy. I believe G-d creates because He is surrounded by a world of automatons, a world He totally controls. Without us, the world is entirely predictable and robotic and uninteresting. And so, G-d breathes His spirit into Adam so that Adam can be like G-d, unpredictable. He is supposed to act in G-d's image and feel the spirit of G-d within Him. He is supposed to come into a relationship with the Divine.

But G-d doesn't *dictate* Adam's path. If he did, Adam would have no independence. Instead, He plants two spiritual rivers. The first of these rivers is called *Pishon*, which means 'spread out'. This implies the river has influence on the world around it. It surrounds a land of change (based on the root *chol*). It has within it good (*tov*) gold with stones of distinction (*bedel* from the root *hevdel*) and stones that connect the human and the divine (the *shoham* stone that brings together aspects of the priests' garments). This river describes a process of creation (G-d calls things 'good' when He creates them), of distinctions and of connection to G-d. And it seems to run in a circle; building virtues upon virtues. This is the great reward of fulfillment in the story.

The other river is called *gichon*, which means 'belly' or 'stomach' or even 'move slowly' or 'slither'. It is a lowly river, representative of base desires and a lack of drive. It surrounds a land called Kush, which can mean 'darkness' or 'inferiority'. Darkness, by the way, is what defines the time when G-d *isn't* creating. Darkness isn't good or productive. This is the alternate, a place without productivity, without goodness and without connection to the divine. It also flows in a circle; but is more like a drain. This is the small joy of inaction in the story.

G-d, like the Gnome, gives us a choice. We can choose to create in the image of G-d and grow continually towards Him, or we can be lazy and shiftless and circle the drain.

Of course, Adam chooses the second path. So, G-d introduces pain and evil and loss. It is better for man to know good and evil and be able to relate to G-d than to know neither and be forever distant. But our failure continues. We are corrupt. G-d brings the flood and then chooses the Jewish people as a model for the nations. But we do not walk in the path of G-d, which would enable us to relate to Him. Thus, our pain only increases.

I can only imagine that G-d watches, pained by our suffering.

Today, we are at a moment of crises. Our will can be erased, we can be erased – or we rise up and walk in His footsteps and find our way into a relationship with the singular Divine. We can walk in the path of G-d. And if we do, then all famine and sorry and loss can be erased. If we do, then the prayers of those desperate for salvation can be replaced by the joy of a relationship with our Creator.

We need only lift up our heads and understand. And then the world can be transformed, and the blessings of G-d can be unleashed.

p.s. I live in Modiin, a city which includes the town of Maccabim. I have never been to Bayt Sira. It is right next door.

Noach: The Salvation of Darkness

The darkness is near total. Only a small torch, carried by my sister Atakilla, illuminates the way. The rancid scent of the tallow that fuels her candle disturbs me. The light from the irregular flames sputter against the smooth stone walls of the passageway. I am the Queen of my people, strong and honored. I have no fear. I have brought myself to this, navigating through a narrow cave on the night of a full moon. As we move, shadows shift around us.

I tell myself that I am not afraid.

We squeeze through a narrow gap in the rock, and then we are where we need to be. The place is a small cavern, but the sounds within it will carry far beyond the walls of the mountain. And the lights from within it will cast ominous and frightening shadows on the valley below. I lay down my bundle of wood, ready for the most important moment of my life. And then I look to my sister, who holds the flame. Her dark skin and black hair seem to flicker in the light of the candle. Both of us are wrapped in the course-woven garments of our people. I look at her, and then I see it, the small and sharp obsidian knife in her delicate hand. Its blackness seems to eat the light that surrounds it. She holds it dangerously, threateningly.

Her smile is twisted with self-congratulation.

I know, in that moment, that she intends to kill me.

My own face fills with an expression of shock and surprise.

"What?" I sputter, confusion carried by my voice. Her smile deepens.

"What's going on?" I ask, almost demanding an answer.

"You, my darling sister Teluklik, are gullible," Atakilla says. Her voice is light and playful and joyous. It is a voice of peace and conciliation, not backstabbing deceit.

I think about throwing myself on the stone floor of the cave, begging for her mercy. But she might attack then. My sister is faster than I am. And her knife, I am sure, is laced with poison.

I'm not ready to die.

"Do you remember when your husband died?" Atakilla asks.

I nod, as sadness overwhelms my expression. The memories flood my mind.

"I do," I say.

"The morning after you were wed, you woke up, but *he* did not. His heart had stopped. He had been poisoned in his own bed."

"I remember," I say, reluctantly. My chance to be Queen had been robbed from me. At one time, that seemed like all that mattered. I wanted to be Queen, the "rescuer of my people."

The title had come from our history. Only a hundred winters before, my people had lived in the wilderness, surrounded by beautiful mountains and blessed by nature. Our men were fierce warriors famous for their prowess in battle. But we battled one another. We fought, clan against clan, to defend the lands we hunted. Our Chieftains were proud men, and this was the cause of our wars. We were blessed by nature but cursed by ourselves.

And then nature cursed us because we did not work the lands, but only stole from them. The rivers began to dry, and the rains stopped falling. Game vanished and wild plants died. Our people began to die. We were cursed by nature *and* cursed by ourselves.

We continued to war, fighting over land that did not produce the natural bounty we needed. We could not forage for our foods.

29

We were helpless in the face of catastrophe.

Our redemption came in the form of a Queen. Our first Queen: Pallua. She stood alone among our people. Her parents were of two clans. Her grandparents of two more. And her husband of a fifth. She alone belonged to *all* the clans. And, in their moment of need, they turned to her. They made her Queen. She united them in peace. She taught them to terrace the land and to plant crops. She taught them to use the water we had. And soon, we were blessed; blessed by nature *and* blessed by man. Because we did not war after that, we had no need for warriors or fortresses or weapons. That is why, in every generation since, a Queen has been chosen.

The Queen of the Five Clans; belonging to all and subservient to none. The Queen of the Five Clans, who would lead them to peace and prosperity.

Of course, every clan sought to raise a Queen in their midst. They married among each other, combining four clans. I was born to be a Queen. I had the blood of four of the clans within me. But it was the Council of Chieftains who chose their husbands; the representative of the fifth clan. Queens had to be unifiers. They had to create consensus and peace. They did not so much lead as unite. And so, the Council assigned husbands to those who would be Queen in order to test them. They chose men who were not only disagreeable, but also rough and violent. It was the final test of a Queen. If she could tame such a man, she could tame our people. We were the people of peace. And in a hundred winters, peace had come to define us.

My sister speaks again, "The Council knew they had chosen a man a wife might kill. It was not unexpected. And you told them that *you* had killed him. All it cost you was your chance to be Queen. They knew you were not a woman of conciliation, but a bringer of death."

"But my husband had not been the kind of man a wife would kill," I say.

"I know," my sister answers. She does know. She was there when he first saw me. Like all those who might become Queen, I roamed through the wilderness, coming to know the world that existed before the time of Pallua. I was exploring the hills near a mountain pass. Atakilla travelled with me. As I roamed, I would find interesting plants and explore their properties. And my sister, three years younger than I, would follow behind me. She watched all that I did, and we spoke often. I loved her. It happened that the Chieftain of the clan I had to marry into was travelling through the pass. And he was not alone. His son Parikia was with him. The boy saw us. He saw me. And in that moment, he fell in love with me. He asked about me and learned I was the elder of two sisters, two sisters who could be Queen.

Up until that day, Parikia had been a good and pleasant young man. But a good and pleasant man could not have me. And so, he changed. He became boorish, and aggressive, and violent. And soon, all who knew him could swear to his poor character and his mean-tempered soul.

He loved me so much he was willing to be hated.

And, when the time came, the Council made him my betrothed. We would be married in a year's time.

In public, Parikia remained the violent person he seemed to be. But in private, with me, he was different. He adored me. He loved me. We had, between us, respect, honor and peace. Not the peace of the Five Clans, imposed by nature and treaty. But true peace, peace which could not be shattered.

I lived to serve him, and he lived to serve me.

We had it all worked out. My betrothed would change slowly, converted by his wife into the man the Council needed to see. It was a simple deception. And when the time came, I would be chosen as Queen. I would lead my people. My sister knew this truth. My sister knew how happy I was to be.

My sister also married from his clan. If I died or if I failed, my family would have another candidate for rule. Atakilla's husband was chosen by our parents and there was no one-year betrothal. His family rewarded ours handsomely for the opportunity to marry a potential Queen. We gained many obsidian tools. We gained the knife she carries this night. But my sister's husband was unlike my own. He had the reputation of a good man. He was smart and diligent. But I knew that behind the stone walls of my sister's house he would beat her. She had no peace.

My year of betrothal passed quickly and then Parikia and I were married. He scowled as we wed under the light of a full moon. All thought they knew the challenges of our relationship. But as we came into our home, a new stone house, the malice disappeared from him. All that remained was love. As the gentle night breeze flowed through the passages of our small house, all that remained was love.

In the morning, he was dead.

"I remember that morning well," Atakilla says, "You told *me* what you believed had happened. You had been eating from a root that granted prophecy and you had confused reality and fiction. You saw your husband as others saw him. And in that world of half-reality, you killed him."

I nod, allowing regret to pass over my face.

"But this is *not* what happened," Atakilla says, "You may have eaten of the root, but *I* killed him. I poisoned him. And I made it look like *you* had done it. I did it so that I could be Queen."

My sister is grinning as she says this, like she's been eager to share this truth for many years.

I just look at her, shock seeming to overwhelm me. But it is anger that I feel. Deep, malevolent anger.

"I thought about killing you too," Atakilla says, "But you were no threat. You believed me. You trusted me. And you felt guilt over a crime you had not committed. When I was elevated to be Queen, you did not protest. You celebrated with me, acknowledging before all that I was the choice that was best for our people."

"I did," I say, my voice quavering.

"But then," a note of bitterness enters her voice, "You deposed me."

"No," I say softly, "I did not. The Council chose me."

"You deposed me," my sister insists, her voice flat. "The Council was manipulated by your allies. All they needed was an enemy. We heard reports of another people's warriors, with women and children, colonizing our lands. And so, manipulated by *your* allies, the Council chose the assassin over the conciliator. They replaced the Queen they thought too peaceful with the gullible sister, they imagined had the will of Death within her. But they were not kind to you. They made you marry the brother of your dead husband. I was delirious with the knowledge of how much he must have hated you. Whatever I suffered with my husband, your suffering must have been greater. The Council imagined they would bring out the worst in you and that you would save them; fueled by your wrath. Perhaps you *were* wrathful. The husband you took vanished. But the Council still did not see the power of *my* wrath."

"But I have done well," I say, earnestly.

"You had a single great idea," she acknowledges with a tip of her head. "On the night of a lunar eclipse you would drug one of our enemy's encampments with hallucinogens. Then – amidst screams of terror and the growl of the jaguar and the shadows of the gods – our men, dressed in the skins of wild animals, would steal their women and children. You would take them to remote villages, distributing them so they never see others of their kind. And you would leave their men behind. You would leave them convinced the jaguar god itself is the ally of our people. Their terror at what they thought they had seen would spread far and wide. And rather than seeking to pillage or attack us, they will bring us offerings. They would sacrifice to us, desperate to harness our power and fearful of our wrath. And we would remain peaceful, as we have been for a hundred winters.

"Is it not a good plan?" I ask.

She smiles, "It is good. But it has a flaw. You imagined that we, in this cave, could fill the valley before us with shouts and cries of complete terror. But play acting will never do. There is no sound like the sound of *real* terror. There is no sound like the sound of *real* death. And without that, all you have planned might fail. So, I am completing your plan. *I* will kill *you*, slowly. And you will scream. In real terror. And the sounds of your terror and your suffering will fill the night and the nightmares of our enemies. And I will live forever, as the Queen who brought peace and power to our people. And you? You will be honored. I will tell the Council you made the sacrifice willingly. But you will die, brought low by your own willingness to trust."

34

She smiles then, a smile of pure evil and of pure triumph. Then she steps forward, ready to carry out her attack. In that instant, I wipe the fear and confusion and sadness from my face. And I allow the edge of a smile to touch the corner of my face.

She hesitates for a moment, confused. And then she stumbles, falling to her knees.

And now it is *her* turn to look up at me, baffled.

Now, it is *my* turn to speak. My heart jumps at the opportunity.

"You were always jealous of what I had. And it blinded you. You saw me, destined to be Queen and you assumed that only *you* could deserve it. You saw me, marrying for love when a Queen could not do that. You saw me getting all that I wanted. And you were jealous.

"You didn't know it then, but I saw you the night you killed my husband. I was *only* seeing reality, not the world of the root I *said* I had consumed. I saw you fleeing after you poisoned the man I loved. I should have stopped you *before* you killed him, but I did not think you would stoop so low.

"After my husband lay dead, I lied about what happened. I lied to *you* so that you would trust me. I told the truth only to Parikia's brother. He also knew that I loved my husband. He knew I did not kill Parikia. The two of us drew close, united by a desire for revenge. I watched as your court was filled with corruption. It seemed to be a court of peace and conciliation. But it was a court of theft and lies. And I knew that if I were to rescue our people, I would have to repair what you had done. I would have to strip away the evil. And so, I sent Parikia's brother away. I sent him to find an enemy and tell them of our wealth and our treasures. *And I sent him to tell them of our weakness.* He would claim to have been a slave for us, plotting his revenge.

"My sister Atakilla, the enemy came because *I* sought them out. And the Council made *me* Queen because *I* knew they would. And they married me to the brother of my husband, because *I* left them all convinced that that brother was my enemy.

"And as the enemy came, *I* knew what they would do. The plan is years old. The timing was chosen by me. I planned it all around the eclipse of the moon. *I* knew that you would plan to kill me. But *you* trusted me, Atakilla. *You* are the gullible one. You let me travel behind you, believing that I would never attack you. You did not even recognize the moment when I did. But I did. I nicked your back with the same venom you used to kill my husband. I did not nick your neck, stopping your heart. I struck the bottom of your spine. It took a few minutes, but I immobilized your legs.

"And now, *you* will not strike me. Instead, *I* will make you scream. And the terror will be real. And your legacy will be a thousand years of peace. Atakilla, you will die soon, but you will live forever as the goddess of our people and as the story our enemies tell of the night they thought to challenge us.

"But I, Teluklik, will be Queen. I will be just and kind, but others will not see it. They will imagine me hateful and fearsome. I will wipe away the corruption you have engendered. I will bless them. And they, in turn, will rule others through terror and through peace. And they will bring peace and prosperity to the world."

My sister looks up at me then. And I can see in her eyes that her screams *will* convince the enemy. In her fear, her candle falls from her hand, igniting the dry wood I brought.

I watch as the flames lick upwards. They will cast magnificent shadows upon the world outside this cave.

Then, as the moon turns to blood in the sky, I step forward.

With sadness and joy and cold determination, I step forward. I will have my revenge. I will be the Queen my people need.

It is then that the terror of a little sister I once loved begins to fill the night.

The setting for this story is the early years of the Chavin people of the central Andes. We do not know their actual name because they left behind no writing. The Chavin people had a major empire that existed from approximately 900 BCE to 250 BCE. But their empire was almost unique in that there were no signs of weapons or fortifications within their borders. It was like those who submitted to them lived in peace while those beyond their borders were too frightened to make war against them. The Chavin people had a central temple, their greatest artifact. It is a massive stone structure which has withstood countless earthquakes. It was designed to confuse. It used light and the sounds of pressurized water and unusual instruments to create frightening effects. The temple was full of statues, statues that all had at least *two* faces. They were designed to confuse. They were male and female and animal and human; all at once.

Those subjects of the Chavin who made pilgrimage to their temple would partake of hallucinogens derived from cacti. And as they travelled the underground passages, their minds would be filled with awe and terror.

Their religion was one of deception.

A much later people in the same region, the Wari, buried their Queens with great pomp and circumstance. And the most famous of Andean people, the Inca, had a moon goddess, sometimes known as KaAtaKilla. Lunar eclipses were said to be a sign that she was being attacked.

I brought all of this together to create an origin story for the Chavin empire.

But the story was not created in a vacuum. It is meant to illuminate the story of Noach.

When I look at the genetic and other physical records, the story of Noach – as commonly understood – seems impossible. There was no dramatic narrowing of life less than 10,000 years ago. The fact that many cultures record a flood reinforces the idea that a flood happened. But it also tells us that peoples all over the world survived it. If we read it carefully, the story *implies* a flood that kills all animal life outside the *teva* (Ark). But it never actually states it. Consider the core three verses of destruction (Bereshit 7:21-23).

The first verse uses the root *gavah*. This word is a precursor of death, "Avraham *gavah* and then died", "Jacob *gavah* and then was gathered." It seems to mean to physically give out. The second verse uses *mait*, which means death – but it is only for those creatures which have *nishmat ruach chaim* – or a living spiritual soul. The last verse uses the root *macha* for the blotting out of all established things. This word is used for a wife who must marry her husband's brother, so he isn't *macha*. It refers to the 'erasing of legacy'. The end of that verse says Noach and the animals with him were the only ones to remain, but this is in the context of *macha*.

The destruction described isn't one of total death. Instead, it describes crushing hardship, the death of those with spiritual souls and the erasure of all legacies. The Chumash uses many descriptions of destruction, but they all contain 'outs'. They all allow the image to be preserved even as the reality can be questioned.

Throughout, the language is intentionally frightening. More frightening than the reality. This concept is strengthened by another curious aspect of the story: there are five dates mentioned in the story of the Flood. The next time a precise date is mentioned involves the taking of the Pascal lamb during the Exodus from Egypt. These dates add an aura of immediacy and reality to the story; just as the rainbow does upon its completion.

Like the story of Teluklik, the story of the flood is initiated by a murder driven by jealousy. Cain kills Hevel and a world of corruption is unleashed – it is a world in which killers are rewarded. The story which follows, the story of the flood, is thus a precautionary tale, meant to curb the worst impulses of man. The great shadows cast by the flood do not lead to goodness, they only curtail evil. Their deception curtails those who deceive. And the violence of the flood rescues all of us from far greater Divine reminders.

The story of the flood saves us from the reality it implies.

Read this way, the story of Teluklik is a parallel to the story of Noach. Murder and corruption are battled by the generation of fear on a magnificent scale. That fear allows blessings to be granted to those who fear Hashem.

p.s. According to Incan legend, Parikia was a god who caused the flood because mankind did not respect him sufficiently.

Lech Lecha: Salt

I can't help but stare in wonder as I watch the army around us make camp for the night. It seemed like we'd been on the move for a week. The entire time, a continual stream of scouts had been coming in and out of the camp, reporting what they encountered to the senior commanders. Baggage trains, supported by little armies of their own, seem to emerge from the land ahead of us, bending towards us as we move. I watch them, and they seem to me like some procession of ants; except instead of taking home some bit of milk or honey, they are bringing supplies to us – the army.

There are tens of thousands of men here, a human mass that seems almost impossible to sustain in one place. But they are being sustained. They've gone to war, they've engaged in battle, and they don't seem slowed or weakened by the experience. The camp doesn't smell of sweat or fear or exhaustion. Instead, wafts of wine and meat barbecued in smoke of native trees seems to drift over us.

This army is a wealthy army, and a fortunate one.

But not all who are here are so fortunate.

The men with me, we are not so fortunate.

We smell like fear.

We are about to die.

And *I* should have seen it coming.

I'd come from the East. I was a young man when I'd left. But I learned what the Easterners could do. They organized huge cities. They ran industries. They operated incredible taxation systems. Their leaders had awe-inspiring wealth. Theirs was a dynamic world. Regularly, new alliances, better at organization or with some slight benefit in arms, would rise to the fore. Borders were constantly shifting. But it was also a static world. Because the elites never changed. It took tremendous amounts of money and influence and power to hold your own in their world. And if you weren't powerful, you would be suppressed. It wasn't possible for new people to gather the resources necessary to stand alone in a world without natural boundaries. In this world, startups played no part. Try to jump into the ranks of power and you'd be slaughtered in particularly colorful ways.

But it had gotten even worse. One man, a master of organization and business, had pulled together an alliance around a simple principle. He would control the market for grain. He had life and death in his hands. Entire cities could be destroyed, and no army would be needed. This man could charge whatever he wanted for his product, and he did. He gathered incredible sums of money and gained the ability to field ever larger armies with better and better technologies.

And his alliance grew. It was increasingly clear that others had no ability to resist.

We called him He-who-surrounds-the-grain.

Everything in that old world was becoming even more calcified. It was stifling. For an energetic young man like me there were only two choices: join the bureaucracy or get killed. Smart young and energetic men weren't allowed to *not* join the team. I didn't like my choices.

That's why I'd agreed when my uncle decided to leave.

Most people in my world don't just move around. If they go to a new society, it is either as soldiers *in* a conquering army or as captives *of* a conquering army. We don't reach across societies or cultures. My grandfather was the exception. He loved to move. He loved to surround himself with new people. I think he had the same problems I do; he just found one place, one culture, stifling. He never stuck around. But he never really got where he was going, either. He never really got beyond the borders of the calcified world. He travelled for a thousand miles and, in reality, end up in the same place he'd started, ruled by the same kinds of men.

My uncle didn't want to stop there. But he wasn't motivated by wanderlust. If he had been, he wouldn't have done what he did. No, my uncle has an inner drive: he loves *people* more than any other man I've ever met. His face lights up with the chance to speak to them. And people love him. They talk to him, and they feel important and elevated by doing so. They feel like he's lifted them up and carried them forward.

All the troubles of the world vanish when he is around.

My uncle is wealthy, but his great power is not wealth or military might or technology. His power is his love of people. Perhaps that is why he is known as "the father of elevation." He was lucky to marry a woman who would protect his legacy, because he doesn't have that bone in his body. Together, the two of them decided that if they really wanted to change the world, they had to leave what they knew. They had to go someplace that wasn't so settled. They had to go someplace that was truly dynamic.

There, they could plant new ideas.

It wasn't like they planned it out, though. My uncle just got the idea in his head that the world would change. And then, somehow, his love for humanity would spread and even the world we came from would somehow shift its course and become a better place. The farmers would be raised up. And the great men would be cowed. And the terrible wars would end.

My uncle has this incredible inner spark. He's a great man. He's also crazy.

Nonetheless, I was happy to leave. With him around, I felt like I'd be okay.

When the time came, we sold everything, bought a bunch of sheep – a sort of mobile wealth – and then we just left.

Things weren't easy at first. He kept calling out in the name of his deity, like he expected a miracle at any moment. But all we got was trouble. We got where we were going, but then we had to leave, almost immediately, for Egypt. It was the kind of place I was used to. Lots of culture. But there, things were *really* fixed in stone. They were led by a Pharaoh who could do, and did, whatever he wanted.

If my uncle's G-d actually has any power, those Pharaohs have got it coming.

Eventually, we made it back to the frontier. Somehow the Pharaoh *paid my uncle* to leave. And then business finally began to pick up. Our flocks grew and things were great. But our employees were fighting. My uncle loves me. He didn't want to fight with me. So, we went our separate ways. Of course, he'd come to change the world. I'd only come to escape the world I'd been a part of. It was only natural for us to go our separate ways. As I looked down towards the Jordan River valley, I knew what I must do. There, in the middle of the deadest of deserts was a city surrounded by verdant green crops. *That* was where I decided to go.

When I got there, the city wasn't welcoming. It didn't take me too long to understand why. They were hiding what they were doing. After all, how can they be growing such incredible crops in a desert?

But they had worked it out. They were taking the water from the Salt Sea into shallow pools and letting it evaporate. They were producing something that *wasn't* salt. They then combined it with our natural urban run-off. And what was left was the most incredible fertilizer I've ever seen. With water from the hills and the river Jordan, they could support tremendous crops.

When I finally understood what they were doing, I knew I could vastly improve what they were doing. It's the Easterner in me. I knew I could scale up their enterprise.

When they finally let me have a chance, we ended up establishing huge stockpiles of the fertilizer. We had too much for our own lands and so we expanded, building up existing cities. The entire time, we were loosely allied with He-who-surrounds-the-grain. He'd sent emissaries to us and rather than go to a war we weren't ready for; we made an uneasy peace. We paid him tribute and he left us alone. But we lied about just how productive we were. Nobody was really allowed to know. As we grew stronger and stronger, we sold grain into his markets without telling him. I was doing exactly what I wanted to. And I knew that when we were strong enough, we'd throw off the alliance. And then we'd be free.

Before long, we'd capture cities of our own and transform them. And bit by bit, our crops would spread, and we would grow as powerful as He-who-surrounds-the-grain.

But our fraud was discovered.

A traveler, a guest brought into a man's house, turned out to be a spy. He worked out what we were doing. And just like that we were forced into a rebellion we weren't ready for.

He-who-surrounds-the-grain swooped in. But he didn't just attack us. After taking the effort and money necessary to form an army, he decided to use it to its fullest advantage. He decided to get rid of leaks in the market. He attacked and burned fields and massacred people. Not our people, other people. It was simple market consolidation, but innocents who were no part of our war paid the price. I heard the reports and I mourned, but what I could I do?

I didn't expect my uncle to be attacked. He wasn't a farmer. Instead, all of us rebels just prepared for the inevitable.

Our cities were bordered on three sides. One by the salt sea and two others by slime pits where the salt waters had receded. We thought that made us stronger. So, we prepared to defend that fourth side. We expected the enemy to use fire, which would have been a catastrophe. A single torch set amongst our fertilizer would have blown the whole place sky high. Knowing this, we set ourselves well in front of the city.

We didn't want it to become a bomb.

But it wasn't burned. When the army of He-who-surrounds-the-grain finally came, it was overwhelming. We had five minor forces from an outlying region, and they had four major forces from the center of humanity. They had incredible numbers. And as soon as we saw them, we knew we could not fight. We also knew we could not flee. We were surrounded on three sides by what we had once imagined were defenses, but which were actually traps. We surrendered, without a fight. Our kings fled, but they were trapped in the pits. A few others managed to make it to the hills. They weren't pursued. It wasn't worth the effort. What could they do?

And just like that, S'dom was gone. He-who-surrounds-the-grain took us all captive. He didn't kill us. He wanted our secrets. He took us, and he took a great amount of our fertilizer.

It was remarkably bloodless; like everything was a carefully executed business transaction.

And now the transaction is almost complete. One of us, predictably, has told He-who-surrounds-the-grain what we have been doing. We have no loyalty, only profit. Any of us would have volunteered, knowing that those who were not first would die. He-who-surrounds-the-grain made sure nothing was being withheld. It took about a week, during which time we travelled north. Into the hills and towards Damascus.

Now, night is falling, and we who did not speak are about to die. Perhaps all of us are about to die.

For some reason, the army hasn't formed us into a line. Instead, markings have been dabbed on our faces and we have been gathered into a tight group in a small clearing in the forests near Damascus. I know the area well; it is only an hour's walk from our old home in Charan. Home might be close, but we are beyond help. We are deep within the territory of our enemy.

Before long, I see our executioners line up opposite us. They have beautiful short bows and almost no armor. I know the armies of the East are based on rapid movement overwhelming the defenses of their enemies. That, and their ability to strike from a distance.

I look at the executioners in the fading light and then I understand the formatting and the markings. The soldiers are barely men and He-who-circles-the-grain misses no opportunity. He is training his youngest soldiers to kill. We are to simulate an enemy formation. And each man has been marked as a single target for each of the young soldiers.

Amid all the excitement, I barely notice the rustle in the shrubs. But it is there. A shadow cast by the moon where there hadn't been one before. Is it an animal? Could it be a person? But who could have come?

Perhaps it is simply another level of training for the boys?

But then the arrows are fired. Not the arrows of our executioners, but others from the bushes that surround them. They are not just arrows; they are arrows tipped with flame. And as they fly, I know where they are headed.

They are headed towards the stockpiles of our fertilizer.

Like one, I and my fellow citizens fall to the ground. And then, moments later, the earth beings to shake with a series of colossal explosions. It is like no sound any man has ever heard. Then the shadows emerge and become men. Not many men, only a few hundred. But in the sudden confusion and the massive death caused by their attack, their sparkling blades cut through their suddenly helpless enemies. They are dressed in our enemy's uniforms, but in a few moments, I know who they are. They are the allies of my father from the land of Canaan.

It seems like only minutes before the camp falls and even He-who-surrounds-the-grain is dead. And then, just like that, the East is left in the East and the West is freed.

When I finally see my uncle, his normally bright face is darkened by the death he has caused. But there is something else there as well. Some sort of sadness. He sees me, comes towards me and embraces me.

"Thank you," I say.

He nods sadly and answers, "I was too late."

I am only confused for a moment. But then I understand. Those other people, those other farmers, died. The Raphaim, the Zuzim, the

Emim, the Horim, the Amorim and the Amalekim. So many innocents were killed. So many died.

And my uncle, the man who loves all of humankind, did nothing.

He only acted when *I* was in danger.

I can't quite explain the revulsion that washes over me. But I pull away from him. He rescued *me*. He helps those he loves, but he does nothing - when the risks are high – for strangers. He is not the man I imagined him to be. He is not the lover of all mankind.

He could have helped, but he did nothing for the innocents.

He doesn't pull me back towards him. He doesn't argue. He just asks, "Are you going back to S'dom?"

And in that instant, I know I am. My people were betrayed by a traveler. They were betrayed by a spy. They will slaughter any stranger.

My uncle pretended to care about others. He pretended to care about the innocents. But he did nothing for the Raphaim, the Zuzim, the Emim, the Horim, the Amorim and the Amalekim.

I will do better. I will rescue the foreigner. I will even rescue the spy.

Because the stranger should not be set above one's own kin.

We travel together, back towards our unsettled lands. But our split is inevitable.

Never can the two of us be brought back together.

This story was remarkably difficult to write. I tried to write proxies for it from Avram's (whose name is later changed to Avraham) perspective. I set it in contemporary urban neighborhoods, in Benghazi and even on Mars. I tried to focus on Avraham's perspective. But all of those were just a simple transfer of the Torah's version of the story. Nothing would be added. Avram is a man who travels to a new land to make a difference. He is motivated by the opportunity to change the world in a place where the rules are not yet firm. G-d promises him that he will be a blessing to the families of the world. He is like many who make Aliyah to Israel, escaping the calcification of societies that had previously hosted our people.

Lacking any benefit in changing the setting of the story, I decided simply to change the perspective.

As I see it, Avram makes a difficult decision. He chooses not to help Amalek and the others. He only helps his kin. In an era in which we are surrounded by wars and tremendous cruelty, his choice is incredibly relevant. Do we intercede in the catastrophes along our borders? It is a difficult question.

In the end, Hashem reassures Avram that he made the right choice. But Amalek believes differently. They dedicate everything, for evermore, to revenge. They can't forget or forgive. If this was in Amalek's character, then perhaps they should not have been rescued? But how could Avram have known he made the right choice?

I've struggled with this question. How can you choose not to intervene when innocents are being threatened? I even wrote a book, *The City on the Heights*, proposing a way to help without simply going 'Team America' on the aggressors.

Ultimately, the challenge Avram faced is core to knowing G-d. G-d does not impose the good. Avram's tool was relationships, and Hashem's is as well. Avram reached out to those around him, establishing webs of relationships. He wouldn't stand up for Amalek, with whom he had no relationship. But he would stand up for Lot. And if Lot would stand up for others and if that web were to grow out like some fractal of love, then those who would attack it would find themselves isolated and weak. Aggressors can then be crushed and reformed.

Today, we call this a *civil society*.

Avram didn't stand up for Amalek because force in support of a stranger would not build a lasting relationship. Those who are bent towards the worst interpretations, as Amalek was, will find them. They will claim Avram wanted their lands or their property. They will claim it was simply PR. They will claim he had no good intentions, beneath it all. We Jews are all too familiar with those who will interpret everything through the lens of hate.

Building relationships between man and G-d does not require the vision of a prophet. All that is needed is the aspiration and trust in the Lord Almighty. Like Avram, we can spread kindness that lasts thousands of generations. And we can, ultimately, extinguish the hate that takes hold in the cultures of those who cannot forgive.

This story is dedicated to a man in my Kehilla's extended community who passed away the week I wrote the story. He visited our community somewhat regularly and he always took the time to speak to me. He was full of life and joy, and he lifted you up just like I imagine Avram must have done. When he died, I was surprised. He seemed healthy to me. He never said anything to the contrary. I thought that it must have been a surprise. Then I went to his funeral, and I discovered another truth. He'd been battling stage 4 cancer for 18 years. He was incredibly ill. But he did not share that with me. All he shared was joy.

Like Avram, he started with a love of man and learned trust in G-d. Like Avram, he must have been challenged by the hardship of his reality. But he loved those around him. And then he became religious, and he moved to Israel to live out exactly one year of his life. I believe he moved because he was hoping to continue to spread his love to those around him, in the homeland of his people.

His name was Michael Libman and I hope you can join me in continuing to spread his joy; despite the hardship that may mar your own lives.

p.s. Today, the Dead Sea once again produces life-giving fertilizer.

Vayera: Medicine

The camp was dark and smelled of unwashed bodies, dried blood, sand and feces*. Over us, sparsely-leaved trees hung, blotting out much of the night sky. A campfire flickered over our little community. All around the fire were children, their cold AK-47s resting tightly against their sleeping bodies. Nearby, I could just barely make out the sound of a small river flowing – cutting its way through the thin underbrush.

I shouldn't have been awake. I wasn't supposed to be awake. But I couldn't manage to sleep. Once again, I couldn't manage to sleep. I just lay there, my eyes closed, *pretending* to sleep. Pretending the horror had not overcome me. There were no guards watching us. My pretend sleep wasn't fooling anybody else.

I was just trying to fool myself.

The camp, aside from the crackling of the fire, the gurgling of the water, and the shifting of restless bodies, was silent. And then I heard something. I heard soft footsteps. The footsteps of an intruder.

The footsteps of an enemy.

I opened my eyes, grabbed my gun, and rose to my feet. And all around me, like zombies coming to life, other children did the same. We were ready for the enemy. We had no fear of the enemy.

What could you possibly fear if you sought death itself?

We spread out, long practice yielding its benefits on this unlikely battlefield. Were these government troops, coming to kill us? Our eyes and ears focused on the source of the sound. And, slowly, incredibly, it became clear. There was no army, these were the footsteps of a single person.

Who would approach our camp? Who would have the courage? We were feared and hated. We even feared and hated ourselves. As we waited, curiosity rippled through our ranks. A few glanced nervously in other directions, long experience telling them to anticipate a trap. But then, from the thin brush, a woman slowly emerged. She was dressed in a reed skirt and a thin brown cotton top. She had nothing in her hands and only a look of hope on her face.

Nobody shot her. We just watched her, fascinated. And then, without fear or even defiance, she began to look at each of us in turn. Her eyes were yearning for *something*.

I watched her with all the rest, stunned and confused.

And then, in a flash, I realized I *knew* her face.

I *knew* the crazy, fearless, bull-headed woman who walked into our camp.

She was my mother.

And I knew, in that instant, that my worst nightmares had once again been given life.

I was ten years old when they came. There had been nothing special about that day. My father and I were standing knee deep on the banks of the lazy brown river. We had been working. In the distance, I could see the sporadic acacia trees, their vast canopies seeming like green clouds placed against the clear sky of the savanna. Nearby stood our village, a ramshackle collection of tiny brick-walled homes covered with thatched roofs. It was surrounded by the sandy and claylike dirt that defined our world. That was the smell that day and almost every other. Clay and sand and the tepid life of the river.

These were not fertile lands.

In this place, only one useful crop survived: cassava. The plant seemed like a reflection of our reality. Its roots are tough, coated with a thick and protective bark. It can take hold in unforgiving earth. It provides tremendous nourishment; giving us the energy that we need to survive. And it constantly threatens our lives.

Cassava is not like other crops. Lurking within it is a poison. Eating the root raw can be enough to paralyze or even kill a man. And in times of drought, no preparation seems to make it safe. In our tiny village, three women and two children are victims of konzo; their legs have been made useless by the poison within the cassava.

That one plant represented the constant entwinement of our needs *and* our fears.

Our village didn't plant the sweet varieties of cassava. Those required little preparation before they could safely be eaten. But they often needed better earth than we had. And when they did grow, they attracted thieves and bandits. They were a temptation to the desperate wanderers who roamed through the savanna. No, we planted *bitter* cassava. It was loaded with poison, but it discouraged thieves. Few would take the time necessary to safely prepare *our* crop.

And that was why we were in the river. My father and I had knives. We were cutting the bark from the roots and then slicing the roots themselves into small round slivers. Other children were arranging those pieces in the river, submerging them just upstream of a log that prevented them from being washed away. We would soak the cassava here, for hours. And then we would withdraw it, grind it and spread it on large flat mats. The sun would take the final step, its powerful glare hopefully leaching the poison from our food.

My mother was not here. When my mother was in labor with me, she became very, very ill. Everybody in the village knew neither she nor I would survive the labor. The elders began to say prayers for the dying. And then, on the river, a small group appeared in a boat. When they got to the village, it was clear that they were a small travelling medical team. There was a doctor on their boat as well as supplies, a few nurses and a few guards.

The doctor wanted to set up her temporary clinic before she began her work, but the villagers forced her into action. And the doctor saved my mother's life and mine. My mother would never have more children, but our lives had been spared. And they had been given purpose. My father saw the doctor's arrival as a miracle. He saw it as a sign. And he prophesized that *I* would grow up to be a doctor. My father had been a quiet, unassuming man. But he convinced the entire village of his vision. I had been rescued by doctors so that I could be one of them. That's why, while other villages harvested cassava as they needed it, we planted and harvested far more than we needed. And while we planted, my mother traveled. She brought our cassava, processed into safe flour, looking to trade it for goods that could eventually be traded for gold. She traveled often, despite the danger.

She felt G-d had given her life for a reason. She was fearless in her dedication to my father's vision.

Slowly but surely, we had gathered a small stockpile of gold. It was ten years of surplus, buried under my family's small hut.

And, like every other day, we were working so that I could eventually go to school.

We were working so that I could become a doctor.

A little girl saw it first. A small dust cloud in the distance. A few minutes later, we could all see people walking. And then, in terror and dread, we came to realize *who* they were. They had a single all-terrain vehicle. And they had guns. They walked in a loose fit group. And most of them were children.

There was nothing we could do.

We couldn't run fast enough to escape the all-terrain vehicle. And even with our small stockpile of gold, we lacked what is needed to survive in the open savana.

Like automatons, our little community gathered the cassava we'd been preparing and made its way out of the river. We were all there, in the center of the village, when the little army arrived.

I remember every second of what happened next. *Everybody* was forced to kneel in the dirt. And then boys were selected. Boys like me. And we were handed guns, one by one. Pistols. And then we were told to kill our own families. The first boy, Akurungu, refused.

As he watched, they killed his kneeling family.

Then they shot him as well.

They continued with the next boy. And, tears in his eyes, he used the pistol on himself.

We all watched as the armed children in the little band killed his family as well.

I was next.

I wanted to die with my family then. But my father looked up at me with those incredibly intense eyes. And he said, "you are not meant to die today." I shook my head, refusing to believe what he was asking me to do.

I knew the calculus. *They* were going to die. *I* was the variable. But I didn't want to live if I had killed them.

My father gripped the end of the pistol and guided it to his own head. And I looked at him and I saw the pleading in his eyes. He had worked so hard for me. He had worked so hard for his vision. And he would not let me disappoint him. And so, I did what I had to.

I did what he demanded.

Minutes later, we left the village. Almost everybody I knew was dead. Vultures were circling overhead, and I knew the hyenas and wild dogs were not far behind. Before long, nothing would be left of all the work we had done and all the life we had celebrated.

We travelled after that, from village to village. 'Recruiting' just as I had been recruited. We wanted to bring those proud boys down; those boys with families. We wanted to show them they were no better than we had been.

Again and again, we killed. And when enemies were near, when there was some sign of armed resistance, our commanders would force us to sniff some crystal powder. And then in a rage of fury and energy, we would fight. We fought wildly. And those who survived learned how to fight effectively.

All of us became the evil we most hated and feared. All of us did to others what had been done to us. And all of us wanted to die. But we would not kill ourselves. Without exception, our families had died so that we could live. We would not debase their deaths with our own suicides.

That was the only thread of decency that remained within us.

I had grown up in a village that celebrated hope. It had been a village that celebrated *me*. It had been a village that wanted me to escape from it, so that they could take pride in the work I would do.

Now I was in a different place. And there was no escape. The world outside knew what we had done. We could never be accepted again. And if we tried to escape? Then we would be tortured and killed by other children. We'd be brought low by those who lacked the courage to run.

Over time I learned our commanders had once been just like us. I guessed that they, like I, had come to peace with their first great sin. They could not hate themselves for that. But they could, and did, hate themselves for what came after.

Every night we all shuffled restlessly in our camp. We were together, yet so far from one another. Scenes replayed in our minds, individually. Nightmares of the horrors we had inflicted.

And every day we rose again, stealing and killing and recruiting as we had always done.

As time passed, I grew to accept that my father had been wrong. Akurungu had been right. It would have been better to have died that day. My father had desired my life, but the price of my survival had been the lives of so many others. I knew it was a price that was not worth paying.

Nonetheless, day after day, we all paid it. Day after day, the price we paid grew and grew. And it inevitably became an investment. We clung to our own lives ever more fiercely, seeking to give some kind of meaning to all we had taken.

Two years had passed. I had killed thousands and we were a thousand miles from my home.

It seemed like the nightmare would never end.

And then, *my* mother walked into our camp.

We all watched her, stunned by her bravery. And then she saw me, and her face lit up with unquenchable joy. She smiled broadly and said clearly, "My boy, my dear, sweet boy."

I looked back at her with hard eyes. Trying to will her to run. There was no hope for me. There was no reason to love me. I was not the child who she had last seen.

Somehow, she had found me. *Somehow*, she had tracked me down.

And now she was to join the ranks of my nightmares.

"Mama," I said, "You should not be here." I put every ounce of warning into my voice.

And she answered, simply, "My boy, you are to be a doctor. It is time for you to leave."

I couldn't imagine the insanity. How could I leave? How could *she* leave?

Those old dreams were gone now. They'd been replaced by a new reality.

Why had she come?

I stared at her. And I saw the look in my commander's eyes. And I knew what the order would be.

I stepped forward. Towards my mother.

And I raised my rifle.

She looked at me, with no fear in her eyes. And then she looked at the camp.

And then she said, in a voice radiating warmth and love, "You all still have a home."

We stared at her, blankly. And then the first stirrings of hope began to whirl around the camp – as tangible as the wind.

"You are all," she continued, "Still loved."

It was then that I saw tears enter the eyes of those around me. Even those of the commanders.

"Kill her," my commander said. His voice was shaky; he was holding on to a reality he did not want.

My finger moved towards my trigger.

My mother did not look at me then. She looked only at the others.

And she said, "With me, you can *all* have a second chance."

I closed my eyes, not wanting to watch her die. And then I heard it. The sound of rifles dropping to the dirt. It spread furiously. And then it stopped. And I stared at her with shock and confusion. And then I lowered my own rifle to the ground.

And nothing happened.

In that moment *my* mother – who could bear no more children – became mother to us all.

My mother, my fearless mother, had found the bodies of the villagers when she'd returned. She'd understood what had happened. She dug up our little collection of gold. And then she set out in search of me – following our little band from village to village.

Despite all the horrors she saw, her love never left her.

She brought us from the bush, unarmed and unharmed. We expected the world to reject us. And many did. But many others just wanted a second chance. They wanted a second chance with children who had been lost and who could finally be reclaimed.

In the weeks that followed, we lived off the gold she had recovered. Soon after, *our* mother found international charities willing to support us. She bought a small compound in the capital.

We all live there, a band of real brotherhood replacing our army of regret.

We all live there, and we all go to school.

Every morning we rise and say our prayers. *Our* mother glows as she watches us.

And every morning, as we begin our schooling, she smiles over us.

Despite all the horrors she saw, her love has never left her.

And we all know, it never will.

My father's dream is still alive.

Imagine yourself in the shoes of Avraham. You live in a world of violence and destruction and sin. And G-d comes and claims to be able to change all of that. But you struggle to believe.

If He *could* change the world, why hasn't He?

The story of S'dom speaks to this challenge. When the angels explain their mission, they say: "the cry of them is waxed great before the Lord, and the Lord has sent us to destroy it."

The city is crying out for its own destruction. Thankfully, we must search to find a modern corollary. And we can find one. We can find it in the very modern experience of child soldiers in the Lord's Resistance Army.

When you have been compelled to sin and then have forced others to do as you have done, you will grow to hate yourself. When you exclude all others through your violence, you can form an entire society that cries out for its own destruction.

This is why there are no men in Zoar willing to act in the normal way with Lot's daughters. People in this society want the pleasure of intercourse but they do not want to bring new life into their sinful reality. This is the only world Lot's unmarried daughters know. To their credit, they desire a future. Raised by Lot, they do not hate themselves; despite the horror he had almost imposed on them.

The cry for destruction is not enough to condemn S'dom. There must be a test, a verification. When the angels come to S'dom, they create a test. Lot cries out for their survival, a lone moral voice in a community gone mad. But *everybody* – men, women, old and young – joins in their society's evil. Lot, even though he is willing to give everything for these strangers, is unable to turn back their evil and their self-hatred. They cannot change course. Likewise, the mother created a test. If her voice had faltered, then her son could never have been rescued.

S'dom fails the test, but it is the *last* society destroyed by G-d.

The birth of Yitzchak brings an end to this era of the Torah.

As I read it, the entirety of the Torah readings of Lech Lecha and Veyeirah is teaching us about G-d so that we can have a relationship with Him. It is teaching us so that we can share this relationship with the world. Through our fear and acceptance, we can be empowered to bring goodness and holiness to all those around us, just as the mother's acceptance of her husband's vision empowers her to rescue her son.

Ultimately, even Avraham accepts this reality. If there are fewer than 10 righteous men, then there is no kernel to rescue a society like that of S'dom. The establishment of the good is ultimately *our* responsibility; but that responsibility is ultimately dependent on relationships.

We cannot do it alone.

The seed that was planted with Avraham and cultivated with Yitzchak and Yaacov and his descendants is still flourishing. In our day, through our fear and our acceptance and our love, even the victims of the Lord's Resistance Army can be saved. The children in their armies are being disarmed and reintegrated. They face many, many challenges, but some have even gone on to university.

But we must remember that the recovery of these soldiers is only a *reaction* to sin.

We should aim higher.

Through our relationships, we can create a better reality.

We can create a reality in which the nightmares never have a chance to become real in the first place.

---

* The use of the word 'feces' is intentional. It is meant to highlight the distance between this camp and a holy military camp as defined in the Torah.

Chayei Sara: Amazon

I felt the smile leap around my little group. There was no real cause for it. I just looked up and met the eyes of Auiya and I saw the joy there. And she, my oldest friend, saw the joy in my eyes. And then we looked at the others and we realized we were all sharing the same feeling. Pure joy. There was no exclusion, no backbiting, no clawing for status. Just joy. In that moment, we were together, as the elders had always wanted us to be.

That morning, a once great tree had been brought low by a mite. Like so much of the downwind forest, it had been infected long ago – by us. It had stood, dying, for years. And then, with stone axes and ropes and brute force, the men had pulled it down. The crack of the great tree's trunk was stunningly loud as it finally gave way under the pressure of our collective effort. Then, the tree lay dead on the ground, ready to be put to its final use.

Our little cohort of young women had grown up together. We'd started with the basics. The first task I can remember us doing is carrying fruit. Our little team of girls gathered into pairs and lifted baskets of fruit, carrying them from the trees where others picked them to the darkened huts where they were protected and stored. Others directed us, telling us where to go and giving us advice on how to carry our loads. That was the beginning. But, slowly and surely, our challenges grew. Sometimes, we would gather fish from the ponds mankind had engineered alongside the river. Sometimes, we would grind the paste every person wore to ward off the insects that dominate our world. Gradually, we grew more and more independent. We were proud of our cohort. The fifteen of us were a capable team. In some ways, we were more advanced than any of the other groups of girls.

We didn't know what to expect when the tree had been brought down. We didn't know *why* we were there. We assumed, once again, that it was to watch our elders at work. To watch grown men and women do what had to come next. But then the elders had spoken. And they had pointed at *us*. And we knew that we had been chosen. And then the elders did something extraordinary.

They asked everybody else to leave.

We were going to do this alone. Despite all our work and learning, we never expected to be allowed to do something *this* important. There was an almost palpable energy then, as we realized what was going to come next. Once the men and the women and the boys were gone, I gathered our little group together and we got to work. First, we moved around the fallen tree, piling the brush and broken branches near the center of the fallen mass. Everything had been infected by the mite we had killed the tree with. None of it could be allowed to come close to our orchards. None of it could be allowed to threaten the trees that gave us life. We did our job conscientiously and carefully. And proudly.

And then we moved on. A runner fetched a small flame from the flame-house and we encircled the tree and then lit the brush we had gathered. The job was simple: char the tree. We had to manage the fire carefully, ensuring that the tree was not turned to ash. We needed only to kill the mites and remove whatever other life had taken hold in the already dead flesh of the tree itself.

It was a delicate job. A good result would be charcoal, uniform charcoal. No ash and no living flesh. So, here, we would add fuel to the fire to encourage more burning. And there, we would pull the fuel away and then smother the small fires with thick and coarsely woven blankets intended for that purpose. The entire time we watched the fire with careful eyes. We had to make sure the mites did not ride flaming embers into our orchards. We burned these trees downwind from the orchards, but sometimes the winds around fires are not so predictable. And so, we would watch the embers and we would chase any that dared blow towards our crops.

As we watched and acted, the fire spread steadily along the tree. We could watch it burn and we could see, with our own eyes, that we were doing our job perfectly. After us, men would come with stone hammers and smash the tree to pieces. Finally, boys would come and carry the charcoal back into our lands, mixing it with pottery and flesh and eating away at the nothingness of the jungle.

Ours was only one small part of this job. But it was important, and we were doing it perfectly. And so, as we watched, the joy spread from girl to girl. And in that moment, we all saw our futures. We knew we'd be together for the rest of our lives, having babies and planting and working and enlarging our world. And then we would pass together and give our work to another generation.

That thought filled my mind. Until, suddenly, I felt myself pulled upwards – away from the fire. And then I saw the forest from high above, as no man has seen it.

When I looked down, though, I saw nothing. Everything my people had created was gone. I could see no trace of us, no trace of our world. No trace of our people. My perspective drew back down into the forest. But even now, my world was gone. Everything was jungle. Somehow, I *knew* I was in a time after our time. And I knew nothing of our people remained.

It seemed so real. So real that when I returned to my world, I wasn't sure I had re-entered it. I looked up and saw the other girls looking down at me.

Their faces were full of care and concern.

"The fire!" I blurted, "We must manage the fire."

"The fire is out," said Auiya, "It has been for a day now."

I looked at her, confused.

"You've been away," said Auiya, "Something happened at the fire."

"Did you finish it?" I asked, "Did you finish our task."

"Perfectly," she said. Then she asked, "What happened?"

I thought about telling her and the other girls who were there. I thought about telling them what I'd seen. But would they mock me then? Would they force me out and exclude me?

What would *I* do to a girl who claimed to see visions of our world erased? Even if I believed her, fear would make me drive her away. Even if I loved her, I would only offer her false consolation.

I would not *solve* her fear. And so, I knew they would not solve mine.

"I think the heat must have gotten to me," I said, "I don't know what happened."

In a way it was true.

I got up from that bed then, uninjured. And I talked to the girls about the fire and about our great success. They were worried about me, but I shared none of my own fear. I acted as if nothing at all had happened. I knew I needed to talk to someone, though not to the girls and not to the elders. They did not like change, or new things. Who could say how they would react? And not to my mother or to the men of our place. They would not understand. I needed to speak to somebody who could help me push back against the nightmare I had encountered.

Eventually, we stopped talking about the fire. The excitement was replaced by simple contentment and not a little worry for me. And then, as night came, the girls lay down to sleep. I told them that I was not tired; I had slept for a day, after all. Instead, I began to walk through the world. I wanted others to see an aimless girl wandering at night. But I was not wandering. I was seeking a target.

I was seeking Tekeo, the strangest man in the world.

Everyone in the world worked together. They built the sluices and berms that trapped fish – together. They planted trees – together. They pushed back the jungle – together. They harvested and built and carved and cooked – together.

But Tekeo did none of these things.

From when we were small children, Tekeo was different. He didn't play with others. He would wander, fearlessly, stupidly, into the jungle. He would explore, by himself, beyond the edges of the world. The elders wanted to stop him. They wanted to make him useful. Then they discovered that he was useful. He found new seeds, new insects, new parasites, new animals. He brought things back; things that the world could use. He was only 15, but we learned a great deal from him.

He made our world stronger.

I went to Tekeo because he alone knows about the world beyond the world; so he alone might have an answer to my nightmare. I went to Tekeo because he alone is not a part of us; so he alone will share what I tell him with others.

In the middle of the night, I came to his small home. He did not live *in* the world, but on its edge. The elders feared diseases he might carry. His house was dark, without fire. I opened the door and snuck in, quietly.

I thought perhaps I would escape attention, but instead I heard a whisper, "Naia?"

He knew I was there.

"Yes," I said.

I could almost hear a smile when he answered, "I am glad you have come."

I skipped any formalities. I told him why I was there and what I had seen. And I asked him what I must do. He listened quietly and patiently. And then, when I was done, he spoke.

"Naia," he asked, "Have you ever wondered what would remain should the jungle overcome our world?"

"No," I said.

"Everything in our world will vanish," he said, "Our trees are just trees, they will mix with the species that live in the wilds. The river will wash away our berms and sieves. Our thatch homes will be consumed by the jungle. And our bodies will be overwhelmed by insects and humidity and rot. We build with life. With death, everything we create will disappear. Nothing will remain."

I stared at him, beginning to understand.

"Your vision," he said, "Is of what will be left when we stop planting and harvesting and clearing."

I just stared at him. Everything would vanish. And I *knew* it would vanish. I had seen through the eyes of those who would never know we had existed.

"What do we do?" I asked.

He sat there, thinking for a long while. He did it like it was the most natural thing in the world. Just to think, without speaking to those around him.

Eventually, a smile crossed his face and he said, "I have an idea."

We stepped outside his hut. And under the cover of darkness, we began to dig. We dug and dug, an enormous hole in the ground. And when the sun came up, we were stilling digging. The people began to come and watch us and wonder what we were doing. But Tekeo did not explain it.

He said only that it was something he had learned from his explorations.

We worked for weeks, our hole getting deeper and wider and longer. For those weeks, I did not work with my cohort. No one criticized me. But, bit by bit, I knew I was growing apart from the women who had defined me.

And then, after weeks of labor, Tekeo turned to me and asked, "What do you see now?"

I stared back at him, confused.

"Close your eyes," he said, "And think of the future. And tell me what you see."

I closed my eyes and thought of the future. And once again, I was pulled away from myself. Up into the sky above. But then my vision changed. The green trees turned to colors: red and oranges. And then, in an instant, they were gone. And I saw the grey earth below. And there, drawn on the canvass of the land was a dot. Our hole. I opened my eyes. Tekeo was there, waiting.

"I saw it," I said, "Our hole has survived, below the overwhelming foliage of the jungle."

He just smiled. And then he said, "I think that is what our people need."

Tekeo became my prophet. He told the people then of what we were doing and why. We told them of the future. He told them of the messages we would create, to tell the people who came from above that we had once been here.

The elders were angry. Our world was perfect. All were fed. All were happy. Why did we need to think of the future? But we kept digging, and slowly others joined us. They too wanted some part of themselves to survive.

Bit by bit, we built greater and more complex designs. And I would check them, viewing them from on high, knowing how others would see them. And Tekeo testified to the truth of my visions. We became leaders of our people. But we were no longer a part of them. We were priests, separate from mankind.

It was worth the cost. Our people acquired something new. They acquired meaning. We began not only to live – eating the fruit of our garden – but to leave our footprint on the world. We would no longer simply pass away, leaving no trace of our lives.

And I began to love Tekeo. It was he who had made my nightmare become a dream. It was his wisdom that had reshaped the reality only I could see. Before long, Tekeo and I married.

It was then that he told me there were *other* worlds, other places mankind had carved out of the jungle. Before he met me, he had travelled between them, sharing wisdom between peoples. We both knew what we must do. And so, together and alone, we travelled across worlds. And we brought the people who lived within those worlds' knowledge of the future. We shared the *idea* of the future with them.

And everywhere we went, Tekeo lovingly guided the creation of designs only I could see.

And slowly, bit by bit, I watched the jungle fill with the stamp of the people who lived within it.

In time, we had a daughter. Like us, she belonged to no world. She was dedicated only to the future.

Decades passed. We grew old together, honored by the peoples of the jungle as we hobbled between their worlds. They saw wisdom and meaning within us. And we saw it grow within each other.

And then, while we were travelling between worlds, Tekeo fell ill. He had never been ill before. Somehow, he knew his end was coming. And so, we took one final voyage; we travelled back to our world, the place where we had been born.

We stopped on the edge of that place, surrounded by the dead trees that marked where our orchards would next expand. And there, on the edge of our world, Tekeo grew sicker. There, on the edge of our world, Tekeo died.

The villagers came then. They wanted to help bury the great man. They wanted to take part in his final chapter. But I knew I alone must honor him. It was the greatest honor *I* could give and the greatest honor he could receive. I prepared his final resting place. It was a bed of coals and pottery; materials that would lock in the nutrients of his body.

He would be made a part of the pottery and coals; so that he could be reborn within the fruit that feed our people. In that moment, though, it did not seem like enough. It seemed like he deserved more.

I knelt there, my daughter beside me. I knelt before the body of the man I loved. The moisture of the jungle filled my lungs, and the buzzing of insects filled my ears. I knew I had never been so aware of my present. I looked at him, trying to find a hint of the wisdom that had once filled his eyes and the strength that had once filled his arms. But his eyes had been made hollow and his arms had been eviscerated by death.

I closed my eyes then. I willed myself to dream. I begged for a vision. I wanted to know what would become of his memory. But nothing came to me. For the first time in many years, there was no vision. There was only me, my daughter and the shell of a man I had loved.

It was in that instant that I understood. Those who will see the jungle from above will know *we* were here. We had told them that. But they will never *who* Tekeo was. They will never know who any of us were. Humanity is not in monuments, but in stories.

So, I knelt before Tekeo, and honored him as only I could. I carved one little pattern in the soil before him. It was a pattern that would wash away in the next rain. No one would remember the pattern, but all would remember that I had drawn it – an ephemeral reflection of a life of wisdom and action.

Soon, Tekeo was joined with the soil, and I rose from before him.

Then, my daughter at my side, I turned towards my old village.

Stories cannot survive in the wilderness.

As I raised my eyes, I saw Auiya, my oldest friend. And I saw her son beside her, a strong young man.

Our eyes met and there was a moment of bittersweet joy.

We had once created charcoal, charcoal meant to preserve the nutrients of the earth. Charcoal meant to sustain our bodies. Now, we would create stories. Stories that would preserve the heart of our people and sustain their souls until the day we vanish from the Earth.

This story is set in the Amazon River basin. In the early years of European exploration, one small Spanish group navigated down the Amazon River. They reported seeing massive settlements along hundreds of kilometers next to the river. But when later explorers came, everything was gone. It was assumed the first explorer had heavily embellished his stories. And so, for hundreds of years, we thought of the Amazon as the world's only unspoiled wilderness. But then, as clearcutting spread, we began to uncover vast earthworks. They were seen first by people flying over them and recognizing the hand of mankind. We call them geoglyphs. And with every discovery, our assumptions have been undermined. We have learned that a population of as many as five million once inhabited this place, and they defined everything about it. From soils made of pottery, charcoal and blood, to trees cultivated so they could produce all the fruits a society could need, these people fashioned a vast reality in a harsh world.

But they had no metal and few stones. So, when European diseases came, everything they made, everything but the geoglyphs and a few scattered remnants of tribes, was ultimately consumed by the jungle. In a world made up only of life, nothing survives death. In this world, one can imagine an existence without past or future. Nothing survives its own life. There is only the garden and the here and now. Everything we know speaks to this reality. Everything, that is, but the geoglyphs. In a way, Naia and Tekeo bring holiness – timelessness – to the jungle. Because of them, the people can dedicate their bounty to something beyond themselves.

Naia and Tekeo are, in their world, a version of Avraham and Sarah. Avraham was inspired by visions. He worked on a vast canvass. Like Tekeo, Sarah acted on a far more practical level. She protected her family and the legacy it would establish.

Unlike Naia, Avraham lived in a world full of monuments. Nonetheless, he too understood that it is stories – carried by a people who will live forever – which endure.

In a way, Avraham builds the idea of history itself. For our people, history is not only about the past. It is also about the future. Only with a past *and* a future can you see yourself as part of a greater story. Only with a past and a future do the children of Avraham find meaning in this world.

When Sarah dies, Avraham no longer wrestles with vast ideas or histories. Instead, he engages with the smallest and most basic of concepts. He buries his wife in a cave, not a glorious manmade tomb. He reserves the honor of her burial for himself, refusing to have her legacy hijacked by the likes of Ephron. Through his actions, he creates an enduring memory. That of the holiest of men honoring the greatest of women. It is the *story* of her burial, not the gloriousness of the structure, that makes that cave holy even today.

But he does not stop there. Through Eliezer, he arranges the marriage of his son. As with Naia's daughter, Yitzchak is brought back into the human world. The boy must establish the future, not with timeless monuments or incredible gestures, but through the simple act of marriage.

In the end, Avraham's does not act on the scale of nations or stars. In the end, he acts on an individual, personal, level. Ultimately, this is how the past is woven into the future and the future into the past.

In Parshat Bereshit, mankind is told: "In the sweat of thy face you shall eat bread, until you have returned unto the ground; for out of it you were taken. For dust you are and unto dust shall you return."

It is Avraham who changes this reality. And it is through *us* that his work is continued.

Through stories and ideas, we create the past and establish the future. Through stories we give meaning and light both to those who have returned to the earth and to those who have not yet been born.

p.s. This story is dedicated to the memory of the 11 killed by a terrorist in Pittsburgh and to the memory of the family of 8 wiped out on Israel's Highway 90 by a driver allegedly under the influence of drugs.

Toldot: Felix

The day I first met my husband, we had already been married for seven years.

I remember where I was then. It was a pier in Midtown, part of the New York Ship Passenger Terminal. The place was full of people waiting for arrivals from Europe. Behind us, the traffic on the new West Side Highway was scurrying by. There were so many people there, at the Terminal, excited and worried. They were there to meet loved ones coming from the catastrophe that was left of Europe. Despite the diesel fumes from the ships and tugboats, and the gas from the cars, you could still smell the worry in the sweat of those around me. What would the people coming off the ship be like? Would they be the same people we'd known before?

That last question applied to most of the people there. But not to me. I'd never met Felix Langer. I had no idea what he'd be like. I didn't really care. My plan was a simple one. We'd meet and then we'd get divorced, just like so many other wartime couples.

And after that? After that, life would move on.

Of course, that wasn't how it worked out.

Back in 1937, when I was 17 years old, my father had been a Professor at Columbia University. He was a Classicist, quite a respectable position in those days. But it was my mother who was truly important. Her father was an industrialist who had extended a multi-generational family fortune built through the design and manufacture of electrical motors. She was old money, and lots of it. But my mother's interest wasn't Greek or Roman history. It was music. Specifically, she had a love for the violin.

I bring up the year 1937 because that was the year my mother launched her mission. We had been listening to the radio in our living room when a violinist was introduced. Albert Langer was his name, and he was from Vienna. I remember that moment so clearly. I can still smell the warm woolen fabric of our carpets and our chairs. And then, despite the challenges of recording a violin in those days, the radio seemed to fill the room with an otherworldly sense of awe.

Albert Langer was a musician like no other.

I enjoyed the radio program and then it faded to the background. It became a pleasant memory. Perhaps at some point, Mr. Langer would perform in New York, and I would go to see him. I would like that. I was seventeen and I didn't really know what was going on in Vienna. But my mother did. She knew that Mr. Langer, a Jew, was in mortal danger as long as he remained in Austria.

So, she did something only the daughter of a powerful industrialist would think to do. She arranged for the City University of New York to offer Mr. Langer a position. He and his family would have a refuge. They could escape the coming hell. People in our circles didn't exactly love European Jews. Going to such lengths to rescue one was unseemly at best. But she did it anyway, risking herself for a man she'd never met.

She mailed Mr. Langer. And a few months later we got his response. He wrote a letter back to my mother, thanking her profusely. I still remember the exact words he wrote next:

"I apologize, but I feel I should not be treated differently just because I have been blessed with music. As I'm sure you can appreciate, music isn't just technique, but soul. And to have soul, you must live a life of true sincerity. If I take advantage of my music, leaving my community to suffer without me, I abandon sincerity. And if I abandon sincerity, my music will die."

And that was it. He turned my mother down.

Well, it seemed like that was it. But a week later, we received another letter. This one was from Albert Langer's wife, Klara. Her only son Felix was 18 years old and he too needed to escape. She included a photograph of a handsome young man with a complex smile.

The woman pleaded with my mother to find a solution.

And so, she did.

I was the solution.

I was to marry the boy, without ever meeting him. He'd get a visa, as my spouse, and be welcomed to the United States. I went along with it. The way I figured it, with a father like Albert, Felix was probably a pretty good catch. And even if he wasn't, I would still be saving a life.

My mother launched her mission with the fury of a woman who had too much time on her hands. It wasn't an uncommon condition for women of her class. She had a friend who filed 'modified' paperwork. It showed that Felix and I had met and married on a previous trip. A trip Felix had never taken. Then she browbeat another friend in the Diplomatic Corp to get a visa to Felix, as quickly as possible. The US Embassy in Berlin issued the visa and then had a courier deliver it to Vienna. The courier left November 9th, 1938. They arrived November 10th, the day after Kristallnacht.

But that day, neither Felix, nor Albert nor Klara were anywhere to be found.

Soon enough, the war started. A few years later, the embassy closed, and Europe went completely dark. My mother was taken during the war years. She died of cancer. I put aside my own suffering though. I knew so many others were suffering so much more. Then, as our troops finally advanced through Europe, news of the camps began to spread. I remember the horror then. I didn't know the man, but I was consumed with a conviction that Felix was dead.

I needed to know if that was true.

So, on VE Day, May 8th, 1945, while nurses were kissing soldiers in the street, I got back to work. Albert and Klara had vanished. But I found Felix at the end of that year. He was freezing in a D.P. Camp. But he already had a visa, and he already had a wife in the US. My family had resources. I had resources. Within a few weeks, I got him out of Europe.

I went to the pier that day, his photograph in my hand. I was hoping to meet my husband and finish the kindness my mother had started.

I just wanted to rescue him from the D.P. Camp and leave him to live his own life. Then I saw him.

He looked almost as he had in the photograph. At least on the surface. But his face was weathered in a way it hadn't been before. He'd aged far more than seven years. His eyes were filled with the most remarkable emptiness I'd ever seen; like he was staring into a world of nothingness. When he looked towards me, I almost fell over with the shock of it.

And then he saw me, and he somehow realized who I was. And in that moment, I saw something else. Something besides emptiness. In that moment, I felt like I was the only string connecting him to this world. In that moment, I knew he *needed* me, like no man ever had, or ever would.

I had expected Felix to be a musician. But he was another man, at least by the time the war was over. He changed his name to Frank and took *my* last name. Almost as soon as he arrived, he went into business. He didn't pick something glamorous though. Instead, he saw enterprises that had once been sustained by war collapsing all around him. With a small loan from my own fortune, he bought a bankrupt uniform-manufacturing factory for pennies on the dollar. His client was the army. It was a business *everybody* knew would fail. But he was cheap enough, and his investment thrifty enough that he made it work. And while the competition was collapsing, he expanded his offerings to police forces, factories and even the US Postal Service.

His business, through sheer grit, determination and good luck, blossomed.

He made, within a few years, a hundred times what we had put in.

Others were jealous of him, but he was unrelenting. If the powerful pushed into his space, he'd move. But he always found a new wellspring of profits.

Then, in 1949, Felix and I were blessed with two children. Twin boys. With money and power and a young family, we had all the trappings of a great post-war success. People didn't even know 'Frank' was Jewish.

But, despite it all, Felix was not a happy man. He pretended to be. He would take some shallow pleasure from cars and from houses and even from me. He embraced the physical world. But that was all. But I knew, from the emptiness and the need, that there had to be more.

I had expected Felix to be dedicated to his remarkable father and his remarkable music. But he never mentioned his father. And he never listened to music. There was *no* music in our house. No music was ever played at parties or business meetings. And despite the scientific popularity of Musak as a driver of productivity, none was played in his factories.

I put a concerto on once, just to bring something into our home. But Felix flew into a terrible rage, throwing dishes and smashing a vase in his sudden anger.

Oddly, his violence convinced me of the one thing it was meant to disprove. It convinced me that Felix still had music within him.

He had it within him and he was running from it.

As our children grew older, it became clear how different they were. One of them, Robert, was like his father. He was masterful with money. He could see money, feel it – understand it. But he didn't run a factory. He went into finance. As he put it once, he loved to *hunt* money. Building, like Felix had, didn't interest him. He loved the feeling and freedom of financial conquest, not the attachment of hard assets. He was proud of his father and joyful in his pursuits. He while he had some tough times, Felix eyed him almost jealously. The joy Robert found in money was something to behold. And it was clearly something Felix wanted.

His brother David couldn't have been more different. David would run from the house, and hide, just so he could listen to what his father prohibited. He became a musician. Felix pushed David away. He denied David the fuel he needed to flourish. He wrote David out of his inheritance, and he drove David from our home. But David would not be denied.

Sadly, while his technique was phenomenal, David lacked the soul of his grandfather. Somehow, I knew he would never meet with the great man's success.

Then, in 1963, Felix was diagnosed with cancer. There was little to do about it in those days. It was a death sentence. It didn't help that Felix refused any sort of chemotherapy. He had an incredible fear of chemicals. Quickly, he got sicker and sicker. Before long, he was confined to his bed – a rail-thin man who looked like he was once again in the camps.

It was then that his mind began to go. He began to have conversations with me, thinking I was his mother – Klara. And I learned so much then. I learned that his mother had wanted him to leave Vienna. But Felix had agreed with his father. He could not take advantage of his gift. He too had responsibilities. He too should be *with* his community, not escaping from it.

I watched Felix relive the moment when his mother told him he was to be married. He would have new obligations now, obligations to a wife. Felix had been angry then. He had felt betrayed.

And then, days later, all of them had been taken.

I learned about the horrors of the war, as Felix had lived them. His sleeping nightmares became waking nightmares. His eyes darted around the room in terror. And, in snippets, the story was revealed. His parents had not stayed with their community; they had been murdered within days of Kristallnacht.

But Felix had hung on. Felix had survived. He had lived through the darkest hell mankind could create, and he had survived.

He survived, but he was not undamaged.

It was his father's sincerity, his soul, that had locked them into the Holocaust. Felix had once believed in that sincerity. He had believed in his father. And they had been given over to a fate worse than death. After 7 years, Felix had learned to hate all of it. Most critically, he learned to hate music, because he had been sacrificed to it.

That was why Felix ran from his father's music. His father had said that without sincerity there is no soul and without soul there is no music. Felix was willing to give it all up.

As I watched Felix dying, I know there was another truth. He was willing to give it all up, but he had no life without it. I had to return his music to him.

So, I did what my mother once did. I falsified documents. I created a fake will, notarized and witnessed by a court, that dedicated all of Felix's assets to me. It was designated as a repayment for my original loan to him.

And then I left that falsified documents on my husband's desk. As I planned, it was Robert, the son who loved money, who found it.

He came to Felix then. My husband was dying in his bed, but Robert flew into a rage. He was angry, crying, crazed. And all of it was about the money he thought he had lost. He cried about *money* to a man who withstood the Holocaust. And then, mourning his loss and awash in his own pity, he left; angry and disappointed and somehow empty.

I watched my husband then, looking for some sign of understanding. I hoped that, on some level, he would see that a life dedicated to money is no life at all. But as I sat there, watching him, nothing happened. Nothing seemed to pierce his failing mind.

And so, I acted on my own. I called David, my musical son. I asked him to come with his violin.

He was uncertain when he arrived. But I told him to play. So, he put his bow to his instrument and he began to play. As had always been the case, his technique was remarkable. And as had always been the case, his music lacked soul.

But then I saw, at the corner of Felix's mouth, the slightest of smiles. And David saw it too. And it seemed to flow from Felix's face to David's hands. And David's music changed. Not the technique, not the sound, but the sincerity. The soul. And in a glorious cycle, the smile spread over Felix's face and David kept playing. And their souls began to fill the room.

Felix opened his eyes, then; for the first time in days. And I saw, for the first time since I had known him, that there was joy within them.

David saw it too.

He kept playing.

Then I was back in my mother's salon. The smell of wool was all around me. And the radio was playing Albert Langer's remarkable solo.

I listened to them both – Albert and David. And I was filled with joy.

I closed my eyes then, feeling everything.

And then, after what seemed like forever, the music stopped.

When I opened my eyes, Felix was gone.

I looked at his lifeless body and I smiled. I smiled because in that final moment before his death, I had finally met the man I had once married.

In the generation that survived the Holocaust, many Jews denied G-d's existence. But others were *angry* with Him because of the horrors that had been unleashed. Their ancestors had clung desperately to their Jewish identity, despite the risk. And because of their Jewish identity, they had effectively been offered up to G-d by their fathers' faith.

We see a parallel to this with the story of Yitzchak (Isaac). When Yitzchak first meets Rivka (Rebecca), we read, in a conventional translation: "And Yitzchak went out to meditate in the field at the eventide; and he lifted up his eyes, and saw, and behold, there were camels coming."

But "at the eventide" isn't exactly a word-for-word translation. Something more literal would be "in the face of twilight." Twilight is a period of uncertainty – neither dark nor light. The word for meditating also suggests prayer; or thinking profoundly. So, the sentence could poetically be stating "And Yitzchak went out to think profoundly in the face of uncertainty."

The last time we'd seen him, Yitzchak had been made a sacrifice to G-d. Afterwards, he had travelled to the place where Hagar's prayers at been answered. But his prayers had not been answered. After all, he could not find certainty. He had been sacrificed by his own father. How could the G-d that promised Avraham the future allow that to happen? How can the G-d who promised us the future allow the Holocaust to occur?

The answer is unclear. And so, we think profoundly in the face of uncertainty.

This uncertainty is the emptiness, and the need, that fills Felix's face when he arrives in New York. It is the same force that drives him towards the physical, towards the material and towards assimilation.

It motivates Felix just as it motives Yitzchak. Yitzchak was the only farmer among ancient Jewish leaders. He craved the stability of land. Yitzchak named wells, seeking his own foothold in the world. Yitzchak, so spiritually fragile, could not leave the land of Israel. And

86

Yitzchak embraced his physical son while rejecting the one who is spiritual.

Of course, life is not simply material. The woman in the story recognizes that Felix needs music. She also knows that music is his only true legacy. And so, like Rivka, she teaches her husband what he refuses to accept. When Esav's *cries* over the loss of his inheritance, Yitzchak finally realizes what's truly important. Only then does he bless Yaacov (Jacob) with the legacy of Avraham.

Only when Robert cries over the loss of his inheritance does Felix somehow accept what really matters: his own father's gift.

In a way, we continue to live out this story. Many Jews are actively abandoning the Jewish people. They are rejecting our unique relationship with G-d. They are cursing their brethren in either an honest embrace of the world's values or a shallow submission to that same world's hatreds. But these Jews are not alone. Other Jews have taken on the mantle of Avraham, raising their own children as members of a hated people.

In a way, we are raising our children as Avraham did, despite the risk. In a way, we are sacrificing them to G-d.

We know the risks; we have seen them.

But we also know that without music, there is no life.

p.s. This story is dedicated to those Hungarian Shabbat-keepers who chose to die together with Jews even though they had the opportunity to be freed due to their distinct heritage.

Vayetzei: Hacker

When the Internet came to life in the 1990s, many people saw it as an opportunity for greater and deeper human involvement and interaction. But that wasn't what happened, obviously. Even as the reality became clearer and clearer, very few people still held out hope for something better. My mother was one of them. She was a programmer and had been in the thick of things in the 90s. Then, it seemed like overnight, the Internet had shifted away from her. In true geek-speak, my mother said she wanted to raise up RHC – Real Human Contact. My father had been a computer genius even then and she hoped that together they could make the world a better and more loving place. Instead, my father tried to start a few Internet businesses, failed and ended up in some medium-end data quantification job. His job was actually exactly the opposite of what my mom dreamed of: he thought up new ways to put numbers on human relationships. Not only that: he was good at it. Very very good. He began to give a score to almost everything around him. And along the way his scoring robbed the life from the very thing being scored. He ended up sucking some sort of fundamental marrow from everything he touched; his family included.

My mother never gave up on her dream. But she grew increasingly bitter and angry woman. That's how I knew her, growing up. She would talk about the Turing test, where a computer is judged to have achieved true artificial intelligence by being able to fool a human into thinking they are not talking to a computer. But instead of talking about the latest attempts to pass this test, she argued that the world had flipped this formula on its head. With short one-liners and click-to-likes, humans had started to behave like computers. The robots no longer needed to do much to fit in. We had fallen to their level. My mother was obsessed with this. She kept telling me I was living a nightmare, but *I* didn't see it. It was just a new reality, and she was part of a generation whose time had passed. So what if everybody was buried in cellphones? That was just what life was like. We had evolved, not suffered some horrible loss of the mysterious RHC.

Then, when I was sitting in class in the seventh grade, the school counselor knocked on the classroom door. She quietly and quickly made her way to my desk. She brought me to her office. And then she told me the most devastating news of my life. A distracted driver in an SUV had crossed into the opposing lane of traffic. He had struck my mother's car. Just like that, she was dead.

I went to her funeral, but I had no grandparents, and my father somehow became more and more absorbed in his technology. There was nobody there to mourn *with* me. I tried posting an update on my profile and while hundreds of my schoolmates clicked sad faces, not one seemed willing to actually comfort me. Even the school counselor had nothing more than platitudes to offer.

Nobody, not one person, bothered to give me a single hug.

I went from denying my mother's nightmare to living it. Without her, I had no Real Human Contact. Nobody around me seemed to realize that somehow *touching* just one person could have more impact than a million hits. I had no idea who to turn to. I would just sit in my room and cry as I watched the world pursue what it could quantify: the numbers. The numbers, the hits, were like a drug, each rolling digit providing a micro-dose of satisfaction.

None of it was real and I needed something real.

I wanted, so badly, to tell my mother I finally understood her. But I'd only understood because she wasn't there to tell. Everything was empty. She had been right all along.

I don't know exactly why I did it, but I started to break things. One lunchtime, I just smashed another student's phone. It was worth hundreds of dollars. Everybody around me was shocked. But it didn't really solve anything. The kid just got another phone. Maybe I'd hoped my father would notice, would pay attention, would think about me. He didn't. All he did was hire a psychologist. Not only that, but he told me exactly how much it cost. Maybe he thought it showed how much he cared, but all it did was *quantify* how little he understood.

The psychologist wasn't any use anyway. She and my father were trying to fix *me*.

They didn't realize that *they* were the problem.

Things just got worse from there. Breaking phones wasn't enough. I had to break something a whole lot bigger.

That's when I started to hack. Somehow, I was going to break *everything*. The world couldn't be left to the quants.

I poured myself into hacking. I didn't want to steal or to cheat though. As I worked, and worked some more, I realized that my goal wasn't just to break the system. It was actually to save humanity. I needed to wake the world up.

I thought about my big attack for years. I thought about exactly what I wanted to accomplish. It was when I was sitting in the school cafeteria, laptop open – surrounded by people on their phones – that I realized exactly what I wanted to do. I started work that very instant. I wasn't going to steal user data or passwords or credit cards. I was going to attack a much softer and much more important target. And, after almost six months of work, my attack was finally ready.

I launched it one September morning. It was on a delay fuse; it had to spread and infiltrate its targets before it would act. But one month later, in the middle of October, it was activated. And it worked perfectly. I didn't go after credit cards. I went after counters. Wherever my code found a database with a hit counter, a like counter, a view counter – it scrambled the data behind it. It scrambled humankind's attempt at quantification.

I thought it was truly clever. For a few days, until the systems were restored, losers would have their voices heard and the popular would find themselves cast into obscurity. For a few days, people wouldn't be able to judge themselves or others by their hits. For a few days, people couldn't monetize their views. For a few days, everything would be how it was supposed to be. For a few days, I could dream of actually talking to another person. I couldn't bring my mother back, but maybe I could find a bit of her Real Human Contact.

But it didn't really work.

Everywhere I went, people were just angry. It was like I'd cut them off from life itself. And they *couldn't* live without their drug. They couldn't talk about anything but the fact that it was missing. There was nothing else to them. And I had accomplished nothing, despite all my efforts. And I knew, even before the backups and the offline storage brought the quants back to life, that the world had turned to hunting me.

They were hunting me, and I had nowhere to hide.

FBI Special Agents came to parent's door three weeks after the attack. I knew I had been found. I tried the very last trick I had in my toolkit. I ran a small batch sequence, and I sent my story to the press – all of the press. Maybe, somehow, I'd get my message to the world.

It was a thin string of hope.

Naturally, they stuck me in a prison without Internet access. I was a minor, and so I was in Juvi. Remarkably, for the first time, I found a bit of what I wanted. Nobody had phones there, nobody had computers. The problem was that the place was violent and vindictive. I was getting a touch of RHC, but not the kind anybody would want. The only thing that rescued me was that *I* was scheduled for trial as an adult. The scale of my destruction had been far greater than anybody else's in that place – at least the way they saw it. Many of those kids had hurt people or threatened people, one or two had even killed. But even in that group, I was kind of a dark celebrity.

A billion hits was a far bigger deal than a single murder; even for those who had no connection to the Internet.

I knew that when I was tried, and when I was convicted, I'd end up spending a long stretch of my life in real prison, surrounded by the kind of RHC I could *definitely* do without.

My dad was my first visitor as I awaited trial. It was a pro-forma effort. His employer wasn't exactly pleased with me. Neither was he.

My second visitor was a journalist. He wasn't from one of the big publications. He was freelance. I talked to him, and he seemed sympathetic. And then he left. And then another journalist came. And another. And soon I was doing interviews every moment I was allowed to. I didn't know exactly what they were writing, I didn't have access to a paper or a blog. But I had a lawyer, and he told me the gist of what was happening.

They'd started profiling me as some sort of destroyer. Then I became a kook. And then, bit by bit, they realized I was selling papers.

They began to cast me sympathetically. It was generating hits. The whole process was steamrolling. I wasn't changing the Internet, but the rules of the Internet were rescuing me.

I was popular, so popular that the Internet giants themselves dropped their civil litigation. It was beginning to look bad. I knew it wouldn't help the criminal trial; I'd so clearly broken the law. I'd also publicly admitted it.

Then, when I went for one of my hearings, something amazing happened. The judge bumped my case back down to Juvenile Court. I would be tried, convicted, and freed in just over a year. After that I'd only have probation.

That was three years without access to a computer.

I was a tougher kid by the time I got out of Juvi. But I was also much better off. I'd sold my story for hundreds of thousands of dollars. I'd made a fortune from other people's need for hits. When I finished high school, I was admitted to one of the best colleges in the country. I had a great story. I was growing by every metric.

Of course, I was just as broken as I'd always been. I was a celebrity, not a person. I was a billion hits in human form. And I was totally alone.

I thought about online dating, but the whole system was falling apart. People couldn't get to know each other from data packets on a screen. There was no humanity in it, not in most cases. People needed to meet. But they were losing the ability to get to know each other. They didn't know how to act. They didn't know what was normal. They didn't know how to talk like adults, even if they were. They were all so lonely. And so, I decided to do what my mother had once done. I decided to connect.

I logged on one day and I announced an invitation-only event at a local coffee shop. I rented the whole place out. Fifteen people registered and fifteen people showed up. They'd come to see me, the Internet celebrity. But I didn't give them me. I did something else entirely. I grabbed one person from the crowd, at random. And then I brought him up to a little stage. He sat there, uncertain about what to do. So, I asked: "What's your name?"

And, just like that, we spent ten minutes, just talking. And everybody just watched. And the whole room got to know somebody they hadn't known. When he left the stage, others approached him. Some found they liked him, others didn't. But they began to *talk*. They began to talk to him and *about* him. Not shallow conversations, but serious ones.

They began to have what my mother had wanted so badly: RHC. I was amazed. After a few minutes I called up a young woman. And she sat down, nervously. And I started the same way: "What's your name?"

And it worked just like it had with the man. And the room was infused with another buzz of activity and connection. The room was full of RHC.

And *I* knew I had something. I founded a business. I called it 'What's Your Name'. I bought online ads, I trained interviewers. I sold tickets. And within two years we had thousands of chapters.

Tens of thousands of people were meeting and talking and getting to know each other.

The Internet was spreading RHC.

Of course, it didn't work for *me*. I was a celebrity, not a person. Everybody already knew my name. And so, nobody seemed able to get to know *me*.

And then one Thursday night, at a small gathering at a coffee shop, I invited a young woman up to the stage. I just knew we'd have a great conversation. She had a sparkle about her. A touch of the mischievous. A touch of the mysterious. I *wanted* to interview her.

Then, right before I could deliver my signature question, she asked me: "What's your name?"

I looked at her, wondering whether she was joking. But there was no guile there. There was no sarcasm. She didn't know who I was. I answered her question. And for the next ten minutes, I answered more and more of her questions. Real questions, not celebrity interview questions. Somehow, through what she asked *me*, I got to know *her*.

Somehow, in ten minutes flat, I fell in love.

When the time was up, I just sat there. And she just sat there.

Then, together, we left the stage.

I have long read this Torah reading in a very particular way: Yaacov (Jacob) desperately wants the birthright. But he isn't seeking wealth or power. His mother convinces him to go before his father because Yitzchak will bless him "before Hashem." We know, from this, that Yaacov is seeking divine connection. He realizes that Esav (Esau) will not honor that connection and that the true inheritance of his forefathers will go to waste.

Nonetheless, Yaacov's approach almost leads to his own destruction. He doesn't just ask his father for a blessing. He lies to him and tries to replace Esav. He breaks all of the rules. He destroys convention just as the character in this story destroys quantification.

But it doesn't work. Before long, he was driven from home, penniless and hungry and desperate.

When he gets to Padan Aram, he continues on his law-breaking path. He lifts the stone over the well, breaking a convention that protects the society from thieves like Lavan (Laban). He has not learned to honor convention. But he does learn. It starts when Lavan takes him in *because he is a relative*. He takes him in because of social convention. And in the reading that follows, there are at least 19 different contracts. Some are implicit, some explicit. But Yaacov learns to accept and then use them. When Leah is switched for Rachel, Yaacov accepts that Leah should be married first. It is a convention that justifies breaking the contract he thought he had. When Leah buys his attentions from Rachel, he accepts her contract. And, bit by bit, he learns to use contracts – explicit, implicit and social – to his own advantage. When Lavan tries to cheat him from his wages, he uses the explicit contract to take everything Lavan has. And when Lavan accuses him of theft, he uses the standards of shepherding to defend his actions. Just like the men in the story, he learns to use reality to rebuild reality.

Yaacov goes from a man who would burn everything down to accomplish what he feels is just – to a man who uses everything the world has to deliver a more fundamental justice. He is like a firebrand of a young revolutionary who loses everything and then realizes he can be more effective by using the systems he decries to create a better reality. He goes from being a simple young man who dwells in tents to being the only one of the forefathers who builds a house.

We all go through the process of being young firebrands. We all think we can change the world. It fires our imaginations. But almost all of us fail. The world is setup to defend itself from radical change. Almost all of us emerge from this period in our lives defeated by reality. We give up on change and just accept reality, like the protagonist's father. But that is not the only path. As Yaakov's story shows us, our acceptance of the world as it is, is the very key we need to reinvent it.

Vayishlach: Siblings

Michael's Story

It all started in a bar. The place had all the touches. Dim lighting. The smell of some wood polish. A scattering of mass market mementos that were meant to look cool. And the sorts of perfect lines and surfaces that told you this was a mass-market beer-flogging chain, not some place full of real history and relationships. But... they sold beer. And my brother Liam and I liked beer. We weren't craft types, we just liked beer. And so, as was our custom, we were hanging out having a few.

Then our lives changed, forever.

It was pretty innocuous at first. These two women came up to us. One was beautiful, her name was Chloe. The other wasn't much to look at. Her name was Emma.

Back in our hometown, I might have been a bit suspicious of Chloe. Our grandfather was an oilman with the kind of fortune considered vast in that kind of place. He had north of $50 million dollars. We were his only two grandkids and our parents weren't beloved by the old man. Liam loved that money; it gave him such a boost being the grandson of such a rich man. For my part, I loved the old man himself. He was a coot, kind of a throwback to another reality. He was great to talk to and hang out with. So, we were it when it came to a destination for all that money. In that town, women even came up to *me* all the time. Liam and I were a chance to strike it rich, or at least live like you might for a few days. Just trying to date us was like buying a lottery ticket and not knowing whether it was *the one*.

But, in this city, we were total unknowns. Nobody was playing for our money. The beautiful one was interested in my brother, for all the obvious reasons. The other was just tagging along so Liam's 'friend' didn't interrupt things between us.

We'd been in this rodeo a few times before. Nonetheless, *this* time my brother didn't react with the normal flirtatious "you've got me for a few days" kind of thing. He reacted with something a heck of a lot more potent. He actually stuttered once. For my part, I talked to Emma and she to me. Turns out Emma and Chloe were sisters. Emma seemed to like me, but it was really a one-way thing. Somehow, though, all four of us decided to go out on a double date. Two brothers and two sisters.

I didn't know why, but from the get-go, it didn't seem like a tremendously good idea.

Time hasn't changed that assessment.

But we went out. And Liam – his born name is Leonard – pulled out every trick in his book. He was *into* this woman. And before the month was out, they were engaged to be married. It just blew me away.

Emma and I were still puttering along then. But then my brother got this idea that *I* should also get engaged.

"Marry her, marry her, marry her." My brother just kept repeating it, time and again. I was luke-warm on the subject, but that didn't stop him.

"I don't find her terribly attractive," I told him once, although I was ashamed to say it – being as I was sure I'd often been on the other side of that particular assessment.

"Good!" said Liam, "You *shouldn't* marry a looker. *You* aren't a looker. A looker won't be satisfied, her priorities will be in the wrong

99

place. And she'll, let's say, find *other* targets for her affections. This girl's not a looker. But she's good. She's kind. She's focused and goal oriented. And she loves you. Her being a bit ugly is a good thing."

He was right. She was good and kind and focused and goal oriented. And she liked me.

"You're marrying a looker," I'd argue.

"Yeah, man," he'd say, "but I *am* the showboat. I'll keep her busy."

I just laughed.

"Listen," Liam would say, "I am sooo happy. I just want you to have some of what I've got."

I didn't have what he had. I knew it. But eventually, I sort of gave in. On some level, I guess I didn't want to let Emma down. She was a good person. So, the four of us got married in this big double wedding.

I remember the day. Liam and Chloe (born name Claire) were all over each other.

Emma and I were more reserved.

But everything was kind of cool between the four of us.

At least it was until my grandfather died.

Emma's Story

"Do me a favor."

Those four words redefined my life.

We were in a bar and Chloe pointed out a guy. He was *gorgeous*. Not really my style, but definitely hers.

"What about him?" I asked.

"He's with a friend," she said. I knew what that implied. Chloe needed a friend to go with her. Normally, we'd let the men come to Chloe. Men like a challenge. Normally my job was fending them off.

This time, though, *she* wanted to act.

I really didn't know why, but I agreed. And it worked. She really hit it off with this gorgeous guy, Liam. Somehow, she managed to play coy despite making the first move, I'll never really understand that magic. The funny thing was, I actually liked the other guy, Michael. He seemed decent and hard-working and straightforward. He wasn't really into me, I could tell. Nonetheless, as the weeks passed, I got to like him more and more. I really got into him. But he didn't reciprocate.

Nonetheless, after Chloe got engaged, she decided that I should have Michael, and that was that.

I knew Michael was being pressured, but I was somehow okay with that. The more I got to know him, the more I admired him and wanted him to want me back. I told myself I was willing to settle for having him close. Somehow, she got him to agree to marry me.

We married, but I was incredibly envious as I watched Chloe and Liam at the wedding. They were so in love. And I just didn't have what Chloe had. I was scared that no matter how close I held Michael, I never would.

The brothers' grandfather died not long after the wedding. When it came to his fortune, the brothers were the obvious inheritors. But instead of gifting the two of them equal shares, he gave *everything* to Michael. *Everything*. The will said why. Michael was hard-working. Michael valued things beyond money. Michael was serious. And Michael had loved the old man himself, not just his cash.

That was not a happy day.

Liam was furious. Chloe was furious. I tried to involve Chloe in my life. I tried to invite her into the luxuries I had. I knew she would have done the same for me. But she pulled away. And what else could I do?

Anyway, it turned out I was good with money. We started with $50 million. But I took it out of the oil business and sunk it into a wide variety of investments. Sure, Michael worked his tail off, monitoring and shepherding our investments. But I made the big choices. I was good at it. Within a few years, we had $150 million, and it kept growing from there. I kept hoping maybe it would draw Michael in, but it never did. Our relationship wasn't getting any better.

It was crass, but the way I began to figure it was that I didn't have Chloe's relationship with her husband – so I had to think of the money as some kind of compensation. I was rich. I had a nice car. And I donated tens of millions of dollars to a whole host of causes. Medical research, poverty alleviation, women's shelters, you name it. It was wonderful to be able to help. I didn't feel even guilty when I spent money on myself.

Nonetheless, I kept trying to bring Chloe back. No matter what I did, she just drifted further and further away. She and Liam moved back to his old hometown. And Michael? Michael was just beavering away, watching the money, doing his part – but he barely noticed me.

When we bought a yacht, I invited Chloe to the christening. I wanted her to spend time with me, to get some of the benefits of our wealth. But she showed up drunk and angry. She cursed me. She cursed the yacht. And then it sank three weeks later. I thought maybe there was foul play, but apparently the cause was bad wiring.

I remember when we bought our own jet. We were going to use it to keep tabs on investments. But I could use it for other things. I invited Chloe again – first-class trips anywhere she wanted to go. But I never heard anything back.

And then Michael asked to move back to his hometown. We had over a billion dollars then. He'd never been the most gifted person socially and I didn't exactly fit the profile of a trophy wife. So, I guess maybe he thought his old hometown was as good as anywhere else. Maybe he thought he belonged there.

I wanted him to be happy. And I held out hope that maybe, if things slowed down, we could finally become a real couple.

Come to think of it, I still hoping for exactly that.

Liam's Story

I love my wife. She is the most beautiful person you'd ever meet. But she's also one of the saddest. I guess they go together. When she married me, I knew some of it was about the money. I didn't mind that. The money was part of why *I* liked being me. I was gonna be rich and I didn't mind a girl who wanted to come along for the ride. And she had *some* kindness. She pushed me *hard* to get Ugly Emma married to my brother. She took care of her sister. And I went along. It was worth it. It was all gonna be great.

At least it was gonna be great right up until the point where the money vanished.

You see, that scheming brother of mine, quiet and reserved and stupid around girls, somehow convinced my granddad to give him *everything*. And I got *nothing*. I was furious, but what the hell could I do? I moved back home to be with my equally dispossessed parents.

And the four of us stayed there. Mom, dad, Chloe and me. We were mad as hell as we watched Emma and Michael zip around the world making their billions. Chloe was madder than anybody else. Hell, she tried to take her own life one time, that's how miserable she was.

And then we heard Michael had decided to come on home.

Well, guess what, this was one place he *couldn't* just show up. I had *friends* here and everybody knew the wrong he'd done. So, we gathered at the airport. Near on a hundred of us. We were locked and loaded and waiting for that thieving, greedy, sonfabitch to come gliding in on his private aeroplane. I was gonna kill him, and nobody was gonna give me a hard time about it.

Half the police force and the county judge were there on the tarmac with me.

Then this FedEx truck shows up. And the driver hops out, looking all nervous when he sees all our guns and our mean faces. And he says "Leonard?"

"Leonard who?" asks one of my friends named Leonard.

"Leonard Stewart?"

It'd been a long time since anybody had used that name for me. But I took the bait.

"Here," I said.

And just like that, the FedEx guy handed me this small package. And I opened it up. And inside there was a *certified check* for $50 million dollars.

$50 million. In a check.

And I didn't know what to feel. And the FedEx guy was still pulling away when my brother's jet appeared in the sky on final approach. And I stepped forward. And all my boys stepped in behind me. And I didn't know what I was gonna do.

And then the plane stopped and the door opened and my brother popped his head out and he said, "Liam!"

And I looked at him, still confused.

And he said, "Liam, you came to the airport to welcome me home?"

And I was really confused. And then he walked down the stairs and right up to me and he gave me a huge hug. And he said, "I know you've been upset about the inheritance. We just wanted to make enough that you could have the whole thing, you know. Like you deserved. You've always been such a great brother to me."

And I just felt silly and confused and happy. $50 million dollars was worth a lot more than killing my brother. And so, I hugged him back. And I watched Ugly Emma get off the plane. And then Michael and I went out to a bar while Emma went to the house, they'd bought just off Main Street.

When I got home, I'd worked it all out. I wasn't gonna kill Michael. I might not quite forgive him, but we could move on. I told Chloe about the money, expecting her to squeal with happiness. I wanted her to squeal with happiness. Nothing makes me happier than her being happy. But she didn't squeal.

She was furious.

"That %*&*$ thinks she can buy us off with MONEY!" she shouted.

I wanted to say, "Well, yeah."

After all, money was what this was about, wasn't it?

Apparently, that wouldn't have been a good choice because Chloe went on for another hour or so about how she wasn't gonna be bought off with MONEY. I didn't really follow the argument. Something about a gift not being a replacement for a debt. In truth, I kinda zoned out. But I got the underlyin' meaning. She wanted to destroy her sister, *then* take her money.

Then, about three months later, Emma went ahead and endowed a *hospital*. The town sure had a shortage of medical care. The whole county did. So, she bought a hospital. It was the talk of everywhere. And because she bought a hospital in this rural county with a huge opioid crisis, she decided to build a huge mental health wing. She said it was to help with that very crisis. It made total sense to me.

But Chloe? Chloe was mad. She said it was meant as a message for *her*. Her sister was buying a mental hospital because she thought Chloe belonged in one. You believe that? Buyin' a hospital just to piss off your sister? Who does that?

So, Chloe started throwing dishes. And shouting. But I could tell it was different this time. There was *murder* in her voice. Whatever was gonna' happen, it wasn't gonna' be good.

So, I just up and left. I went out for a beer with some of my boys and I bought a round for *everybody*. $50 million has its perks.

What else could I do?

Chloe's Story

I *made* that *^*%. She was ugly and stupid and awkward, and I got her married to *Michael Stewart*. I knew who the Stewart brothers were even before I walked into that bar. I knew they'd be there.

I used my beauty and my skills, and my charms and I *made* her.

And how'd she pay me back? She didn't.

When she got the money, she didn't give me *anything*.

Instead, she moaned about what a great relationship Liam and I had while she rolled around in cash like an Ugly Pig in you-know-what. Liam was a monkey in jeans. That's who I got stuck with. A poor monkey in jeans.

And Emma thought she could give me gifts to make it even. Trips here and there. Salons. Nice clothes. Rides in her *&^*% Maserati. But I didn't want *gifts*. The money *belonged to me*.

The only reason that she had *any* of it was because I *made* her who she was.

Ungrateful &^*%.

She moaned about Liam and me. But I would have been happy to let her have some of my love, so long as I got what I deserved. But she wasn't giving it to me. I did her a massive kindness, and she didn't repay me with anything.

Then she bought that yacht. A YACHT. Not a dime for her sister mind you, and she gets a yacht. I got real drunk that day. And I went to a bar in town. And I picked up this tough-looking guy. And I convinced him to sink that yacht. I even paid him a little cash to do it.

And he did. Took a few weeks, but he got it *done*. I was happy when I heard about it, *for a millisecond*. Then I heard about the insurance. Ugly Emma didn't lose a *dime*. It just wasn't fair.

This life, living poor with Liam – it wasn't what I deserved. *I* was the beautiful one. *I* was the graceful one. *I* was the one everybody admired. And *I* got nothing.

Then Emma bought her own plane. A plane! I'm working at the burger joint, and my own sister has her own plane. I couldn't take it. Somehow, things had gotten screwed up. When she invited me to fly with her, it all just rushed in on me and I couldn't take it anymore.

That was when I tried to take my own life. It didn't work, but I tried.

Then, a few years later, Emma, Ugly Emma, decided to move to *my* town. She couldn't even let me have *that*. When Liam got together with his drinking buddies – the whole damned town – I wanted them to kill Emma. But, of course, they didn't. Like a nice puppy, Liam took Michael's buy-off and left with his tail between his legs.

That wasn't the straw that broke the camel, but it was close. The final straw? That was when Emma decided to build a mental hospital. It was like she wanted the *entire town* to know she wasn't the one who tried to slit her own wrists. And she was willing to spend tens of millions to do it.

That was when I knew I'd had enough. I screamed and I shouted, and my coward-monkey Liam left the house. And then I called the guy who'd sunk the yacht. And I had him come over. And I told him I'd pay him a *lot* of money to go and kill my sister.

He agreed. He even took a down payment. And then he left. And I waited, like he was a winning lottery ticket, and I was about to get my winnings. But that scumbag didn't do what he promised, not when it came to me. Nothing worked out the way it should've when it came to me.

I realized that as soon as the patrol car pulled up to the front of the house.

Two cops walked up, and they started knocking on the door. And I decided I wasn't going to let them in. I ran off to the living room and opened the gun case. I got out the automatic shotgun Liam is so proud of. And then I marched back towards the front door.

Somebody was going to die.

As I raised the barrel of that gun, I remembered Ugly Emma when we were kids. We were friends then. But I was the one who was going to have the man and the money and the fame. I was the beautiful one people liked. She was the one who was going to hang out in my house and live off the gifts I gave her. It didn't work the other way around. I couldn't live with the other way around.

Somehow, my whole life had gone backwards.

The cops broke down the door just before I fired.

And that's the last thing that ever happened to me.

I've long been struck by Rachel's final action. She bears her second son, but dies in the process. She has time, however, to name him. She chooses Ben-Oni. Ben-Oni is translated by many sources as "son of my sorrow" (Gen 35:18). It can also be read as "son of myself." She was dying, so the sorrow was reasonable – but it is such a *sad* name that you have to wonder whether there is more to it than spur of the moment resignation. Why not choose something ultimately hopeful?

In contrast to this poignant moment, the end of the reading seems long and boring. An entire chapter (Gen 36) is dedicated to the many many descendants of Esav. All 43 verses focus on the descendants of a character who is not the main thrust of the story. The question is, why?

To me, the answer to both questions lays in the relationships between siblings. The first relationship we see is that between Esav and Yaacov. They enter the story at war. As Esav sees it, Yaacov stole his inheritance of money and power. So, Esav shows up with four hundred men, ready to kill. Yaacov defuses the crises by sending his brother extensive gifts and then honoring him when they finally meet. In a way, he returns the inheritance just as Michael does in this telling. Theirs is not a loving relationship, but it is not permanently poisoned by war. Yaacov, Israel, survives the day and Esav is

109

seemingly rewarded with glorious descendants who occupy a prime place in the story kept alive by the Children of Israel. Despite its many challenges, this is a relationship that can be emulated.

The relationship of Leah and Rachel is very different. The Torah describes the two sisters by saying: "Leah's eyes were weak; but Rachel was of beautiful form and fair to look upon." (Gen 29:17) Rachel is the one who snags Yaacov – she is the Chloe. She is the one loved by her husband. But Leah is unloved. She is Ugly Emma. And, almost as compensation, Leah is blessed with a brace of children. And as we see in their names, she is always hoping that the children she brings to the marriage will lead her husband to love her. It is just like the money Ugly Emma makes. It never seems to work.

To her credit, Leah is focused on her own situation. But Rachel seems consumed by jealousy. The desire to beat her sister is so strong it seems to overwhelm her desire for survival. As the Torah writes: "Rachel envied her sister; and she said unto Jacob: 'Give me children, or else I die.'" (Gen 30:1)

Then, when Rachel's handmaid has her first child, Rachel says: "With mighty wrestlings have I wrestled with my sister and have prevailed." (Gen 30:8). She is fighting her sister, not searching for her own blessings. Perhaps she is angry that her sister stole what her own beauty should have secured. She also seems to disregard her husband's love – she's willing to sell it for some flowers. When they flee, Rachel strikes out against her father – who gave Leah to Yaacov. She takes his gods. She robs him of his powers. And she does not tell her husband, perhaps revealing that her motive was revenge, not self-protection. This, indirectly, appears to lead to her death.

In this light of this history, it is not surprising she names her second child Ben-Oni. Perhaps, she looked back on her life and saw only loss. Despite the husband she had and the glorious and good sons she was blessed with, she was sorrow itself. There is no blaze of glory or attempts to physically harm her sister, but the sadness remains.

She had had such potential. But, *in her eyes*, all of it had been lost.

There is a third sibling relationship in this reading, that of Shimon and Levi and their sister Dinah. They are willing to go to war and destroy a city in order to protect something. But it isn't the family's pride or honor. Instead, it is a key concept: they are fighting *tumah*. *Tumah* is the loss of potential. Later, the tribe of Levi is given the full-time job of fighting *tumah*, although primarily through symbolic means.

When I wrote this, the week's reading coincided with the United States holiday of Thanksgiving. In a way, it is fitting. If we focus on beating those around us, and on getting what we 'deserve,' then we earn nothing but sorrow. If we focus only on that which we do not have, we never discover our blessings.

But if we accept peace with our rivals and focus on that for which we can be thankful (while protecting our core purpose), we will be blessed. Yaacov and Esav are both examples of this.

And so, in a way, are we.

When Leah named Judah – from whose name the word 'Jew' is derived – she said: "This time will I give thanks to G-d." (Gen 29:35)

Vayeshev: Wizard

The alley I called home was poorly lit and strewn with discarded needles, food wrappers and the other detritus of homeless living. All of that was bad, but what was worse was the smell. It was a smell of unwashed bodies and rot and of mold. It was the smell of despair. That smell alone was enough to keep those who didn't have to live there far away. That smell didn't stay in the alley though. It came with us wherever we went. Wherever we went, people turned their faces away in disgust. We were marked by our circumstance.

Sometimes, living in that alley, with those people, it seemed like there was no way out. It seemed like the end of the road.

I wasn't the first to live there. There'd been a broken community when I'd arrived. At first, I'd looked at them and I'd thought that I was different. I thought I had nothing in common with *them*. After all, *they* used drugs. *They* came from broken homes. *They* were desperate.

But *I* wasn't like that, was I?

Bit-by-bit, though, I realized that I had more in common with them than I'd realized. The more I learned, the closer my life got to being tolerable. Eventually, I found myself crawling back into my spot in that dim alley, greeting those friends who had made it through another day, and then closing my eyes somehow embraced by the filth of those I considered my neighbors.

Eventually, I realized they had as much in common with me as any other people.

Eventually, I looked forward to coming home.

As you may have guessed, I'm not exactly normal.

I grew up normal. My father was a Minister at a local church. He was a deeply religious man. And he was a man who basically figured that whatever was wrong, G-d would work it out. A lot was wrong. G-d didn't work it out. The church accountant was skimming from the collections, leaving us with barely enough to eat. My mother was deeply depressed and unsatisfied with her life. My father had a major heart problem, which hobbled him physically. It didn't stop him from thinking that G-d would work it out.

When I was young, I thought he was the most righteous of men. People could just feel his holiness. Well, except for those like the accountant who were too cynical to be pierced by his power. Of course, I was his son. How can the son of a man like that not think that his father is right in all things?

I looked up to him, I admired him.

At least until I got to be a little older.

I was about 16 when I realized what the accountant was doing. I didn't know how I worked it out. I thought about turning him in. But, already, I was seeing things from another perspective. I was beginning to think my dad deserved what he got. He let the world walk all over him. Why should I stand up where he had failed to?

The deprivation and sadness and patheticness of my home had driven me away from everything my father stood for. I knew, given the chance, that I'd push back on reality. I'd stand up for myself.

Nonetheless, I somehow found myself sinking into *his* magical thinking. I began to think things would work out if I just wanted them to. There was a difference though.

In my case, it worked.

It was subtle at first. I'd study for a test. And when the time came, I'd sit down and start going through it. And I would know the answers to *all* the questions. I was smart, but for the first time in my life I was scoring 100% on everything. When I got the tests back, I'd known the answers to a bunch of the questions that I'd studied. But there were also those that just flabbergasted me. When I reviewed that I'd done, I had no clue what the answer was. But I had written the answers down, correctly. I knew that didn't make much sense, but I was a teenage boy and so I just didn't think too much about it. I just pocketed my straight As and began to spend more of my time chasing girls.

I was out with some friends late one Saturday night. It was dark and late, and we were on a curving two-lane road. I was driving because everybody else had a little too much to drink. And I don't know why, but at some point, I just pulled over and stopped on a patch of gravel on the side of the road. My friends began asking me what the heck I was doing. And then, 10 seconds later, a semi-truck came barreling around the corner, on *our* side of the road, going the *wrong* direction. The driver shot off the road, right behind us. It turned out he'd had a heart attack. And if I hadn't pulled over, we would all have been dead.

My friends asked me how I knew it would happen. I didn't know what to tell them. Things just worked out.

Then we had our high-school graduation. I went to another friend's party. His dad got up to speak, just to congratulate him. He had no notes, and nothing written down, but I knew every word he was going to say – just before he said it. I just knew, like I could read his mind.

I may have been oblivious about the tests, but this was stuff I couldn't ignore.

Somehow, I was either reading minds or I was seeing the future.

Being a seventeen-year-old-boy, I did the obvious thing.

I decided to become a magician.

I found a comedy club and asked the owner if I could do my act. The guy was almost as cynical as my dad's accountant.

"What act?" he asked.

"I can read minds," I said.

"Hmph," he answered, "What am I thinking?"

"That I can't read minds," I said. I didn't need any magic to know that.

He snickered a bit.

"And now?" he asked.

"That that was too easy."

"You got a decent brain kid; how about now?"

"That unlike me, your girlfriend Amy is kind of dull."

He just looked at me. Then he booked me for a show.

I was so excited! I had two weeks to get ready, not that I needed any props. I had just decided to go around the room, telling people what they were thinking. No fancy stuff, just spit it out and amaze them with what I could do. I practiced on everybody around me – at least within my own head. I got pretty good at getting a fast read on what people were thinking.

And when the big night came, I was ready. I was an unknown act, but they had a pretty famous comedian on later so a lot of people were there. I stepped up on the stage. And I just began.

I pointed at one guy, "Nervous about my act."

Next: "Wondering what I'm doing."

Next: "Something to do with mind reading."

And I just kept going. I recorded surprise, then wonder at how I was doing what I was doing, then amazement. But then there was something new. Fear. People got scared. They began to think about what they wanted to hide from me. But I was showing off my power. And I just kept going. I spat it out, clear as day. Affairs. Addictions. Desires. Lies. All out in the open. And fear. More and more fear. Fear that I wasn't doing a trick. Fear that I was up to something else. The patrons began to flee.

And then the owner of the club, the same guy who had interviewed me, kicked me off the stage.

"I'm doing great!" I protested.

He didn't seem to care. Two minutes later, I was on the street – completely confused.

I didn't know it then, but somebody had violated club policy and recorded my act. It went up on YouTube with the title "Freakiest thing ever". And it immediately garnered views. By the time I got home, there were hundreds of thousands of views. My father had seen it, and he was frightened. Almost like the Devil was in me. He was too full of love to kick me out of the house though.

I went to bed. Half an hour later, my mother woke me up. Her inner thoughts weren't pretty, and she didn't want them shared. As my father slept, she drove me out of the house. I slept on the street that night, for the first time in my life. I still figured it would be okay. I'd sleep with some friends the next day; I had plenty. But by the time I got to school the next day, the video had tens of millions of hits. Just like that, everybody I knew was suddenly scared of me.

I could read minds and all they wanted to do was hide. The principal suspended me because I was disrupting school just by being there. I headed back out to the streets.

I didn't know what to do, but I figured I could do *something*. I could be an investigator. Maybe help the police. I tried, but policemen have secrets too. They didn't want me. And pretty soon I found myself not only homeless but driven further and further away from the 'nicer' parts of the homeless world. I couldn't beg in the good spots or sleep in the best alcoves; I was squeezed out of them all. I managed to make a tiny amount of money finding street junk and then locating people who would be willing to pay for it. I had the edge in every negotiation. But even with a little cash, the only place I could call home was my stinking alleyway – filled with addicts driven so far from society that they were just like me. They were the only people who could stand to be near me.

Then, one night, I came 'home' to find a new face there. There was a kid in our alley. He was maybe sixteen years old. He looked just as emaciated as everybody else there. He was agitated, shaking in some crazy state. But he wasn't high on drugs. Something *else* was wrong. As I looked at his face, and felt his thoughts, I realized he was more frightened than any person I'd ever met.

But he wasn't frightened of *me*. He didn't even recognize *me*.

He was frightened of the world, and he was frightened of the future.

As I probed deeper, and I realized what was scaring him. He'd killed his father. He was afraid of being caught. Most of all, he was afraid of being locked up. I began to talk to him. His speech was malformed in some way. But I could understand him, despite his broken words. I tried to calm him down. I tried to bring him peace. I got absolutely nowhere, though. He was too frightened to be pacified. I knew he needed answers, desperately. He needed to know he'd be safe. He needed to know he would be okay. And he couldn't afford to be lied to.

I couldn't tell the future, though, not beyond a few moments anyway. I couldn't give him what he needed.

And so, I found myself doing something I never thought I'd do. I opened my mouth, and I began to pray. I asked G-d, in front of the young man, for answers. I asked Him for insight. And then, just like that, it came to me. Suddenly, I saw not only the boy's uppermost thoughts, but his entire history. And I saw not the next five seconds, but the next fifteen years.

I sat there, stunned for a minute. The kid in front of me had endured so much pain. He'd been raised in a locked room. His mother had died there, a prisoner of a sadist, when he was three. He had been tortured and assaulted more times than I could imagine. His father was growing older, but no kinder. The boy didn't know the world could be different. He thought this was how it *should* be. But then, in a moment, he just snapped. He killed his father with the old man's own shirt.

He killed him and then he left the room for the first time in his life, and he began to run.

The police had found the old man, I knew that. They'd worked out what had happened, they'd already decided whoever the boy was, he would never face a night in prison. He would never be locked up. They were investigating, but only to help the victim who was sitting beside me.

The boy couldn't understand this. He didn't know the world. He'd been running for almost a month now, growing weaker and hungrier by the day. He needed help. So, I walked him out of the alley and brought him to the detective in charge of his case. The detective recognized me. He was scared of me. But then he saw the boy and asked me what I knew, and I told him.

I was about to leave when I realized the kid *still* needed something from me. I could see his future. I could see his life stretching before him, a never-ending attempt to outrun the horrors that filled his soul. But he didn't need to see that future. He didn't need the horror. He knew the horror. He needed peace. So, I told him where he'd go. I told him he'd be safe. I told him he'd find comfort. I told him he'd never again be locked up. He smiled as he listened.

He smiled, for the first time, because *my faith* made him realize that it would somehow all be okay.

I went home that night. I came back to the alleyway, with its smells. But *something* had changed.

It took months for me to figure anything out. It took me months before I realized that I'd loved helping that kid. He'd had a need and I'd filled at least some part of it. I'd done a service. I knew I wanted to do more. I decided to set up shop on the street. Not far from my hovel was a carless avenue popular with the busker set. You could register with the city to perform there. I did. Predictably, it wasn't enough. I had a mic and one of those small speakers in my collection of street junk. I had just set them up when a local 'enforcer' tried to chase me away. He knew who I was, and he had a crew to support. They taxed the musicians and acrobats that plied their trade there. If you failed to pay up – whether or not you brought in the coins – they made things go badly for you. He was afraid I'd be bad for business.

You couldn't threaten to blackmail a man like that; he'd make you disappear. But you could pay him off in other ways. So, I told him about a girl who found him interesting. I promised a name if he let me perform. I knew he'd go for it; the guy was crazy lonely.

It was enough. Just like that, I started my show.

I didn't try to hide who I was. It seemed like everybody already knew. I just promised passersby that their secrets would remain secret. I promised them they would enjoy the show. Bit-by-bit, a crowd gathered. This time, lots of cameras were out. I hadn't been seen in years, not in this sort of public way. I was a curiosity, albeit a dangerous one. I saw the fear and excitement of those around me.

But I also saw something else. I saw pain.

"My power is not mine," I said, "It belongs to G-d."

There were some guffaws and smirks. But I did have power and they knew it. Why couldn't it be G-d's?

"G-d will give me answers." I pronounced.

A few people turned to leave.

But then I turned to the most pained person of all, and I asked her, "What do you need?"

She lied, predictably. "A car," she joked. But I saw. Her husband was beating her, and she needed escape. I scribbled an answer on paper. I told her which shelter to call. I told her what time to do it, safely. I told her it would be okay. I did not speak of the fear and the pain, I just handed her the note. And the cameras captured her in her moment of shock and then overwhelming emotion.

"Thank you," she managed, with tears running from her eyes.

I smiled, just as I had seen my father do.

She put $50 in my basket.

I moved on. I helped person after person.

Discretely, quietly, in front of the world, I helped every one of them.

Nobody saw the magic, but everybody saw the power of the stories I was telling.

That night I rented out rooms in a flophouse for everybody in my alley. There were showers there. We cleaned up okay. The next day, we were back on the street. Nonetheless, things were looking up. I even found the enforcer his girl, though it wasn't easy.

Then, I went back to work.

People were waiting this time. I gave credit to G-d and I started working. I helped so many people. But, aside from a bit of cash, nobody really did much to help *me*. Somehow, I knew that was because I was offering relief from pain, nothing more. Escape wasn't enough.

And then, one day, the abused woman – the first one I'd helped – came back. I saw something new in her. Not pain, but hope. Then I realized *who* she was. And I knew what would happen next.

As the show came to close, she walked up to me – just as I knew she would.

She told me her name – just as I knew she would.

She told me what she did – just as I knew she would.

She was the White House Social Secretary. Then she told me that her boss was searching for meaning. Not to run from something, but to find something to embrace.

In that instant, I knew I could tell them both a story that would change all of our lives.

Yosef's (Joseph's) early life is characterized by three sets of dreams. In the first, he is the dreamer, but he shares no interpretation. The meaning of the dreams is obvious. In one, the stars (or fortune) of his entire family (including his deceased mother), would depend on him.

In the other, his brothers' need for food would depend on his ability to provide it. In the absence of explanation, his brothers offer their own interpretation. They see the dreams as an expression of ambition and power. They drive Yosef away.

Yosef, like the man in the story, is blessed in all things. But it leads him down a road of slavery, false accusation and prison.

Then he encounters his second set of dreams. He is not simply told these dreams though; he seeks them out – seeing the sorrow and pain of the dreamers.

In this set, a baker and a wine steward approach him. The wine steward dreams that there is a vine with three branches. It is budding and blossoming and bringing forth grapes. He takes the grapes and presses them into Pharaoh's cup. The baker dreams that there were three baskets of bread on his head, but the birds were eating from the topmost basket.

There is an obvious interpretation here as well. Egypt invented bread and exported it throughout the ancient Mediterranean. Canaan, the land Yosef had come from, was known for wine. In three Torah generations, the vine of Israel would grow and flourish and eventually emerge ready to be dedicated to the service of the King. By contrast, in three Torah generations, the fully baked and matured Egypt will have its highest power eaten away by forces from heaven (birds). This contrast between wine and bread is why we abstain from bread on Pesach (Passover), but have four cups of wine at the Seder.

Yosef does not share this interpretation with the dreamers. He credits G-d and then asks for the chance to interpret. And he tells a personal story, not a national one. It is one that speaks of the baker and wine steward but goes no further. He sets the fear of the wine steward aside, but he gives the man no reason to rescue him. He has helped, but aside from gratitude he has provided no motivation for the favor to be returned.

Perhaps Yosef has learned to tell a better story. But it isn't good enough to free him. The wine steward does not remember him.

Then comes the third set of dreams. These are also obvious. A bull represents a nation's will (a common perspective throughout the region). A cow represents its potential (from a reproductive sense). Pharaoh's thin cows eating the fat ones represent a nation losing its potential. The seven thin ears of corn eating the fat ones represent a nation losing its food.

Yosef says, "It is not in me, only Hashem can answer." Yosef then sets aside the first dream, perhaps because *he* is the one who undermines Egypt's potential. Instead, he focuses on the second. And he offers Pharaoh something more than an interpretation. He offers him an action plan. His action plan is tied to the greatest gift of all: purpose. Yosef tells Pharaoh he should act "so the land does not cease." Pharaoh, a man with nothing lacking, can reach beyond his own time.

Through the progression of these dreams, we see three patterns.

First, Yosef moves from giving no interpretation at all, to giving an interpretation, to advising what to do with his interpretation.

Second, Yosef moves from disregarding the feelings of others, to acting in response to them, to learning how to direct them.

Third, Yosef moves from motivating others to hate him, to motivating others to ignore him, to motivating others to act on his behalf.

Finally, Yosef has moved from showing off his own fate, to acknowledging G-d, to finally stating his own limitations. And as he moves, G-d provides him with interpretations – limited interpretations – that serve his needs.

In reality, all of these trends are intertwined. Caring about others is wrapped up with telling them what they need to hear. Telling them what they need to hear is wrapped up with motivating them. Finding ways to motivate others is enabled by realizing our own limits and by giving credit where it is due. And giving credit where it is due is wrapped up with caring about others.

These are all themes I've tried to capture in the story of the wizard.

It isn't enough to have a gift. You must see the needs of others, embrace them, build a story around them and, always, give credit to G-d for the blessings that you have.

Miketz: The Cousins

The lighting is poor in the library, and the furniture is flimsy and cheap. The place has the non-smell of an almost totally concrete structure. I am happy here, though. I'm as happy here as I've ever been. All around me, men are studying. Some are studying law; others are simply trying to learn how to read. But nobody is mocking anybody else for trying to learn. I'm studying too. And nobody is trying to harass me about it. Instead, strangely, I'm celebrated.

It is just about the last thing I would have expected in a place like this.

Everyone here (aside from the staff) is wearing the exact same clothes: prison fatigues. Those who are studying law are hoping to find a way out. Those who are learning to read are trying for a better life once they're released. Then there's me. I've got *Principles of Corporate Finance* opened in front of me.

My name is Billy Lee, and I came into prison without a high school diploma. Now, I'm two months from leaving with my Masters in Business Administration.

The prisoners around me are proud of what I represent.

You have to understand, I didn't grow up in the kind of place where academics were celebrated. I grew up in a small Appalachian county. My parents were small farmers, working a patch of flattish land between the broken hills. They were poor, but at least they weren't alone. It seemed like every nook that could house a homestead did. And most of those places were populated by our kin. We called each other cousins, but that wasn't necessarily our relationship. We just knew we were part of one big family; a big family pushing back against a massive world that wanted to crush us and our way of life. We were mountain tough though. If you had to pick a fight between our family and the world, we knew who the winners would be.

Nobody was going to take us down.

Every day, an old school bus would ramble along the roads, skittering between the rough hills and gulches that defined our lives. It would gather us to the County seat of Scottsburg. We all went through the motions like school mattered, but it was all make-believe. In a place like this, an education meant you thought you were better than everybody else. It meant you were planning on leaving. It meant *we* weren't enough. W*e* didn't like that.

I hung out with a loose collection of boys. We got up to various and sundry shenanigans. But it was education that made us a real gang. You see, back in high school there was a guy named Jimmy. He was a good-looking kid. But what really set him apart was that he was *great* student. The teachers (all imports from outside the county) were all so proud of him. They weren't so proud of *us*. They thought *we* were trash. But they thought this kid could make *something* of himself. And their education began to do what it did to anybody. It made him think less of us. Before long he'd been infected by those teachers, looking down at all us hillbilly trash.

Jimmy became James and whatever his actual crimes, it was all made worse by the fact that we felt he was trying to make us look bad.

It came to a head one night when a crowd of us got drunk, drove up to his parents' trailer and started shooting. The others wanted to shoot *at* the house, but I argued it was enough just to shoot *near* it. That was the only good thing I did that day. In the end, we scared the

&%$ out of that kid. As we watched, he and his parents flew through the front door, tossed their suitcase in their old pickup, and drove – tires churning up the dirt – straight out of the county. It didn't feel quite right, but it was a victory for us. We became a crew, then. *We* knew what we had done, and we relied on each other to keep that secret.

We picked a name then. It wasn't too clever. The cousins became The Cousins. We lived by a creed, although nobody actually had to say it. The creed was this: "Nobody gets ahead of anybody else."

That's why I didn't have a high school diploma. I knew the material. I got all my homework done with no mistakes. But I never let the teachers see that. In class, I said nothing. And when it came time for tests, I flunked every one. On purpose. I loved learning and I was smart. But although I was smarter than Jimmy; *I* didn't let anybody else know what I could do.

I *loved* studying, though. It didn't stop with school. After I dropped out, I got part-time work doing repairs at the prison. The Cousins would hang out all the time. We'd complain about our many troubles, we'd drink, and we'd go shooting (not generally in that order). We might terrorize a few people, but we kept it pretty gentle. They were family after all. We all were.

But the Cousins weren't all I had.

When I had time alone, I still studied. I learned about history of my county. I tried to work out the clouded origins of my own family. I read up on the Civil War and Civil Rights. I traveled in the woods and through the hills, learning about them too. My focus was the rocks and geology. I wanted to understand the past, the distant past. I'd tell people I was huntin', but I just wasn't very good at it (thus the lack of game). All in all, I got myself an education. I just didn't let anybody know about it.

One day, in the woods, I came across a girl. She wasn't from *my* county. As I watched, she scooped a bunch of dirt into a test tube. I asked her what she was doing, and after she got over the shock of me bein' there, she got all flustered – like I caught her in some very inappropriate position. But I *knew* what she was up to. I don't know what made me do it, but I decided to let her know what *I* was up to.

As she watched, I opened my own satchel, and I showed her what I had in it. I showed her I'd been collecting rocks and I'd taken notes about where I found them. I told her about them. Turned out she had a nice microscope at home and was collecting soil to learn more about the microbes that lived in the hills. She worked as a secretary in a medical clinic in the next county over. And just like me she didn't let anybody know what else she was really up to.

We started dating. She knew about my reputation, but she thought she'd found something better in me. And I guess I wanted to live up to that. Eventually, it came time for us to move in together. So, we got married at the County Court and we moved into a tiny clapboard house. It nestled beneath a little mountain with a burbling stream not 200 feet from the front door. It was hillbilly paradise.

And then I found the pyrope.

I had been wandering in the woods when I came across a deep red, almost black, stone. I didn't know what it was, so I set to work trying to find out. I did find out. I had found pyrope garnet. Pyrope garnet comes from kimberlite tubes and kimberlite tubes are an indicator of something very rare and valuable indeed. Diamonds. Now, I didn't have diamonds. But there was chance of them. There'd been a few tiny little diamond mines in neighboring counties before and I thought, just maybe, finding a few more of the little gems could be quite a pick-me-up.

I talked to The Cousins and we decided to spend our spare time looking for diamonds. I showed them what kimberlite looked like. I showed them what pyrope looked like. And then I showed them what uncut diamonds looked like. And we set off for the hills, searchin' for our dreams.

The idea was this, we'd find one diamond and then we'd start crushing and panning for more.

Sue – that'd be my girlfriend – and I also made a simple deal. She'd get cut in, half-half, on my portion of whatever we found. And in return, she'd support me while I searched.

We found diamonds.

It started with one tiny little rock. And then we started crushing and panning, using water from a nearby stream. We just kept finding diamonds.

I told Sue about the initial find, and I gave her a small, raw, rock. The very next thing I did, though? I divorced her. The fact was, she was an outsider, and I didn't *really* owe her anything.

We all went back to digging through that treasure trove of kimberlite – amassing a fortune in dirty, hard, stone. I left Sue in the rear-view mirror. When we took breaks, we Cousins imagined what we'd do with the money. We wanted new houses, new trucks, new guns. And we wanted to dominate the county.

We thought of ourselves as a little hillbilly mafia.

Then, our diamonds started disappearing. One of the Cousins, a guy named Bob (not Billy Bob, sorry), set up a little stand – like he was huntin'. Bob wasn't a clever guy, he tended to get himself arrested for stupid things. But *this* was smart. He was watching our stash from his huntin' stand.

It only took a day before he caught her.

It was Sue who'd been robbing us.

The Cousins didn't want to treat this like they'd treated Jimmy. They didn't want to just run her off. She wasn't one of us, she couldn't be trusted. She didn't deserve the chance to run.

Somehow, she needed to become a lesson to anybody who'd try to take what belonged to us. So, we decided to shoot her. We'd never killed anybody before but needs must. And while there wasn't exactly a guidebook, we thought it was good form to ask if she had any final requests.

She did.

She wanted *me* to pull the trigger.

I aimed the gun at her, but she just stared at me with those curious eyes. They were curious about why I was doing what I was doing. She'd seen something better in me. Maybe she was wondering where it'd gone. Fact was, she made me wonder too. I didn't pull the trigger. I lowered the gun, then broke down and told the others about the deal I'd made with her. She deserved that; it just took me a while to get to it.

In the end, they were okay with it. It was my cut, after all.

We kept building our stash, hoarding it. We weren't really sure how to sell uncut stones. We were okay, though. We didn't *need* to sell.

Then the prison closed. They said something about wanting to find locations with a larger available workforce. In the battle between the family and the world, it was one point for the world.

Just like that our big family needed help pushing back. We needed help, or we wouldn't survive. We needed to start selling diamonds. I volunteered to go to Atlanta. I needed to take care of my people and Atlanta was big enough and far enough to maybe hide what we were doing. I'd read about the Kimberly process, but I figured we could get around it because nobody was really looking for uncut American diamonds. I was scared, but the whole thing went smoothly. I found a buyer. I got an okay price. And we had a buyer for more diamonds when we needed one. Everything was back on track.

At least it was until my idiot cousin Bob called me on my way back to the county. It turned out the IRS had paid him a visit. Without telling the Cousins, he'd sold some diamonds on the side. That wasn't what had tripped him up, though. He'd also bought a brand-new truck, with cash. Just as the county was facing major layoffs.

He'd been nailed for not filing taxes in the past, buying a truck had been stupid. Of course, Bob had been in trouble before. But now his trouble was threatening the entire county. And calling me had just made it worse. Whatever the IRS imagined was going on, now they'd have no trouble tying it to me.

That was when I really began to take responsibility. My Cousins, my family, my county, needed a break. And I needed to give it to them. So, I stopped by a gun store to buy some Tannerite – a binary explosive that goes up when you shoot it with a fast-enough bullet. And I stopped by a drug dealer and spent all the diamond money on a bunch of meth and some test tubes.

I then drove to Bob and – with our cellphones in the other room – I told him to agree to testify against me. And I told him what he should say.

Next, I drove off into the woods. I found a good spot and put the meth out with the Tannerite and the glass tubes. And then I went about 200 feet down the road and laid out my rifle and just waited.

The Feds had my cell phone and Bob had called them almost immediately after the IRS had visited them. I knew they'd pay me a visit. When I heard the crunch of tires coming from down the hill, I fired once. The Tannerite went up, and so did the meth and the glass. And I had the wreckage of a little meth lab all ready for them to inspect.

They arrested me. They weren't looking for diamonds, meth made sense to them. But I was the only cousin who was arrested. I confessed and they carted me off to jail.

The Cousins came to my one-day trial. It was there that I saw something I'd never seen in them before.

Respect.

I knew the rest of the family would get ahead. I knew I had changed "nobody gets ahead" to "everybody but me gets ahead." But it didn't bother me. Our old folk would have the medicine they needed. Our kids would have clothes.

I wasn't just pushin' back against my peers or admitting my mistakes. I was taking care of those who depended on me.

When they closed the bars on me, I decided I wouldn't stop with sacrificing myself. No, I'd follow in the footsteps of Jimmy and I'd get myself an education. A useful education. Unlike Jimmy, nobody was going to try to make me run for it. And the fact was, the family could use an MBA.

When I get out, we've still got to do something with all those diamonds.

We often read this week's Torah portion and focus on the story of Yosef. Yosef who learns marketing. Yosef who grows into a powerful man in another land. Yosef who learned the importance of purpose. And Yosef who wanted nothing to do with his messed-up family. But maybe Yosef isn't really the focus in the story. Maybe Yosef is just a tool.

When the brothers want to kill Yosef – for thinking he's better – it is Yehuda who suggests that they sell him. It is the seed of responsibility. This is just like what Billy Lee (the hero of the story) does with Jimmy. When Yehuda shortchanges and then wants to execute Tamar, he ends up acknowledging his own mistakes – just as Billy Lee does with Sue. Finally, when his father needs Benyamin (Benjamin) to come home, it is Yehuda who sacrifices himself for his family and his father.

In the story of Billy Lee, the diamonds are a stand-in for the spiritual wealth of the family. In a way, the family hoards that wealth, not wanting anybody else to get ahead. In the end, it is Yehuda who violates the principle that holds them back: he allows everybody but himself to move forward.

Yehuda, like Billy Lee, demonstrates true character.

This is why Yehuda becomes the leader of the Jewish people.

In a way, the 'story of Yosef' is really the story of Yehuda. Perhaps we shouldn't focus on Yosef's story of divine blessing, inspired interpretation and unwavering fate. Perhaps we should focus on Yehuda's story of moral growth and personal transformation as the face of a more understandable reality.

Yosef's story unfolds like a majestic divine plan. But perhaps the story of Yehuda, of true personal growth when facing error and hardship, is the one that can more easily transform us.

p.s. This parsha may coincide with Chanukah. On Chanukah, we celebrate the story of another Yehuda. Yehuda HaMaccabi. At the end of the story, the Menorah burns for 8 days on only one day's worth of oil. It seems like such a minor miracle, but it is a critical one. The Menorah, after all, is our recreation of the burning bush. The bush burned with spiritual energy, but it was never consumed. This idea, this vision is of a world of creation and symbolic connection without loss. This vision represents the core of the Jewish people. We exist, as the Jewish people, to bring the Divine reality of the burning bush into our world.

As we light our candles let us keep in mind that we are remembering the values of Hashem and rededicating ourselves to their protection and realization.

Vayigash: Cactus

While the following story contains imagery commonly associated with other belief systems, it is part of a dvar Torah (explanation of Torah). In other words: be patient, there's a point.

The thin green smell of the boiling cactus is strong within the hut. Its moisture coats the walls and ceiling. Its smell mixes with the clean aroma of the bamboo walls, the long-dried and toasted scent of the cogon grass roof and the earthy odor of the rich dirt floor.

The dark hut feels ready.

As I sit, surrounded by the humidity of the boiling vapors, other people begin to enter. While no one had spoken to me, I knew they would be coming. They'd seen me go into the jungle days earlier. My frail body had slowly pushed through the underbrush. Then, I found what I needed for this occasion. I had gathered the cactus that has been boiling for hours. Everybody had smelled that cactus; they knew what was about to happen.

All around my hut are tall, once modern, apartment blocks. They rise 9 floors into the sky around my hut. They are concrete objects; their floors stacked lifelessly onto the earth below. Somehow, they seem insignificant next to my tiny home.

We used to live in a valley alongside a powerful river. I was only an 8-year-old boy when men in strange clothes began to come to our valley. They said it was the perfect place to build a dam. They wanted us to move. Some objected. Many were excited, though. My parents were excited. After all, the men in strange clothes were generous.

135

They offered to let us farm new land they had cut out of the jungle. They offered to share the technology necessary to make it flourish.

They offered to let us live in modern apartments.

I remember when one of the young men in strange clothes walked us through one of the apartments. I remember the adults watching in amazement as water and light came with the touch of a hand. I remember the women delighting in the ability to wash clothes and bake foods without needing to spend hours by the river or hours carefully stoking a cooking fire.

But most of all, I remember the look on the face of that particular young man in strange clothes. For all his pretending to be generous, the fact was that he was disgusted by us. He condescended to us. He saw us as savages to be lifted up by his offerings.

If the elders and the adults saw that same face, they chose to look past it.

As the men in strange clothes walked us through the 'financial analysis' of our annual crops and the value of our new land and apartments, they argued that the bargain was a good one. They were being so generous because the dam would create tremendous amounts of 'electricity', the thing that enabled modern apartments like the ones we were being offered to function.

The land would be put to a far higher use.

The elders and the adults accepted their bargain. The men in strange clothes were being generous. We would come out ahead.

With that, we left our river valley.

As an eight-year-old, I stayed in the modern apartment for exactly one day. Even as a child, I felt revulsion when I touched the faucets or the switches or the machines. I remember my feet feeling dirtied by the floors that had no dirt and my body feeling discomfited by the comfort of my modern bed.

I left in the middle of the night.

I couldn't go back to our river valley; it was being flooded by the filling of the dam. I couldn't go anywhere. All around the buildings, the jungle was thick and the concrete apartment blocks were hours from any city. They were just a collection of buildings in... nowhere. They had a clearing of their own, though. They had a courtyard. So that is where I went.

As a young boy I began to gather bamboo and cogon grass from the forest. I cut the bamboo with wooden tools and drove stakes through it with the trunk of a heavier tree and fitted it all together and tied the pieces in place with strands of tough cogon grass. I created the structure of the hut that I live in today.

Over days and weeks, I gathered cogon grass and wove it into sections that I layered onto the roof of my small home like oversized shingles.

As I worked, the others watched from the windows of their modern apartments. They all knew what I was doing and how I was doing it. But no one really understood *why*. None joined me.

Over the course of a month, I built my home alone. I built a home separate from all humanity; but surrounded by hundreds of my people.

Eighty years have passed since we left the valley of our ancestors. I am the only survivor of those who left. Now, their children and grandchildren come to me. Some of them are muscled and menacing. Others seem wasted away, halfway to a premature death.

I look them over.

"Are you the council?" I ask.

There are fifteen of them. Our population has exploded into the thousands. The young men before me – and they are all men – nod.

"Yes," one of them says. He towers over the rest. "We are the council."

"And what is your question?"

"Should we take what is ours?" the leader asks. "Should we capture the power plant?"

I knew the question would be asked long before he came to me. I have felt it bubbling up through our people over the course of years. But the asking is a part of the ritual.

I nod and then with shaking hands, I remove the boiling cactus from the flame.

As it begins to cool, I begin to sing. The song seems totally lacking in rhythm. It is haunting and in a language so ancient even I do not understand it. Some in the group close their eyes and listen. But none know the words. None have heard it before. It is the song of the oracle and even I have heard it only once. When I was maybe five years-old, the great shaman of our village had brought me into his hut. As the council watched, I heard and then sang the song I now sing. Then I joined that ancient shaman in the drinking of the cactus tea. He said I would, in time, become my people's oracle.

Now, that time has arrived.

As the council watches, I wrap my hands in bamboo leaves and lift the still hot earthenware pot. I tip it up to my lips and I take a sip, just a sip, of the potent cactus waters.

Then I close my eyes.

I feel the tea flow down into my body. Moments later I feel it beginning to transform me. I find myself suddenly aware of negative energies that had been flowing through me. I feel darkness and doubt and fear and sadness evaporate from above me – like water disappearing from a leaf in the sun. I feel joy and confidence and light rush in to take their place.

When I open my eyes, I am shocked by what I see.

When I had drunk of the cactus as a child, I had been an oracle. When I opened my eyes, I had seen not physical people, but a glowing collection of life and energy and power. I understood: this was the council. They were filled with the energies of the world, and they were great indeed.

But there are no great energies standing before me today. Instead, there are only gray shadows and shoots of some evil force running through them.

I look at them, but I cannot understand.

Surely, I am not seeing their reality.

Then I sense something else. I glance upwards and far above me, far above the hut, I see the dancing of spirits in the heavens. Even they seem diminished. I feel myself rising towards them. I feel myself wanting to ask them: "Why?"

I want to ask them "Why are you so weak?"

But I do not know if the spirits can answer me.

They are only servants of the one Most High.

As I rise, I look down towards the concrete blocks, but I see nothing. There is only darkness surrounded by the dimness of the jungle itself.

I rise further and then I feel myself amongst the spirits. But I do not stop there. I rise above them. Then I see something more glorious than anything I have seen before. There is a radiance there, a power I can hardly comprehend. I shut my eyes, trying to lock out its immensity. But it will not be denied. Spasms of geometric patterns explode across my vision. I glance at them, overwhelmed by their power.

I open my eyes, facing the radiance once again.

With that, I know I must be standing before an Aspect of the One Most High.

I look down again, into the dimness of the spirits and darkness of the world below. I find myself speaking, in the ancient tongue of the oracle song.

"Why" I ask, "have the spirits abandoned us?"

The Aspect does not answer me. Instead, I find myself suddenly within it. I feel myself being pulled back in time. As I watch, the world around me blooms with energy and life. The Aspect of blessing and goodness and joy filling it. I find myself coming down to our old village, the village in the midst of the valley. The people glow with energy.

I begin to travel forward, through the seasons. I see the river rise and the people pray to the One Most High for land. And they fill themselves with the spirit of the land. I see the river fall and I see the people pray for abundance. And they fill themselves with the spirit of abundance.

And I see the heat of the summer sun and I see the people pray for the river's return.

And the spirit of the river fills them.

I see them living in the midst of the forces of the world. Of wind and river and land and life and death - all coming together in that valley and its people. They fill themselves with the spirits of the world and the spirits of the world rejoice in their seasons of victory.

The land and the river and the air and seasons had been a part of the people.

But then, there is a change. The people move and the valley begins to fill with the now still waters of the river. The spirit of the river celebrates its victory. Until, in an instant, it realizes it has been trapped.

The people move to the spiritless concrete towers. They chose to move. In so doing, they tore the spirits away from themselves. The spirits grew angry. The people kept their rituals, but they had been emptied. What meaning was there in a prayer for a rising river when they irrigated their crops from a river that was trapped? What meaning was in a prayer for land when the land was never threatened? What was in a prayer for fertility in a world where they fertilized the soil?

The people sensed their loss. They tried to hold on to the rituals, but the spirits would not return. Everything was emptiness. They could not even connect to their apartments and the land they farmed. They owned neither. They lived there by the grace of the government; and the government had no spirit. Mankind had tamed the spirits and the spirits had vanished.

The people were empty. But they could not remain so. A dark energy came over them. It filled the vacuum the land and the river and the wind had left. It filled that vacuum with destruction and waste. It filled it with alcohol and drugs and endless wasted time before the televisions and video consoles the people now had. It filled the vacuum with crime, a vain effort by the spiritless to fill the emptiness of themselves with themselves.

141

The world around them began to crumble.

I saw the land they farmed. It was weak. It had little life force, and it was not empowered by the people. They just worked it, enslaving it and giving it no proper care.

I saw decades fly by as the meager land slowly began to fail. The fertilizers and irrigation could only accomplish so much given the weak nutrients of the jungle. What little life the land itself had had, was gone. And then, it could give no life.

The darkness became stronger within the people.

I find myself back within myself in my hut.

Standing before me are darkness and evil.

I look up towards the great light of the Aspect, but it is already receding, hidden by the weak spirits of the world.

Then, I understand.

I close my eyes again and feel the power of the cactus leave me.

When I open them, I am back in the hut seeing the physical reality but knowing the spiritual one.

The people around me are empty shells. They are facing poverty and they are overwhelmed by social ills. They want a solution. They want to claim the hydroelectric dam. They want to claim it as their heritage and right.

They imagine it will give them what they need.

They want to fight.

The young men before me respect the traditions. They came to me because of it. But I know now that they can never understand what they had and what was lost.

They can never understand what it meant to be their own masters.

They can never understand what it meant to be at one with the land – growing towards it as it grew towards them.

I know they will not listen to me. They will not even hear my words. The respect they pay me and my words is respect for tradition, nothing more.

When I speak, I know I speak to emptiness.

"You will fight," I say, "You will win. But all you will gain is the production of the plant. All you will gain is the payments from the government. You will get nothing that you truly need."

The leader of the council just looks at me, hearing of victory and disregarding my warnings.

"Then," I continue, "a few months later, the army will come. The army will slaughter you."

The leader of the council smiles and says, "Then we will destroy the plant, and revenge the loss of our heritage."

I say nothing to him. I just sit there in my eighty-six-year-old body.

I know that when the slaughter comes, nothing will be lost.

No matter their conquests, the men before me will remain nothing more than the empty shells of the men their parents and grandparents had once been.

Our people will vanish.

But nothing will be lost.

When you read the story of the Exodus, you can't help but be shocked at the suffering of the Egyptian people. The Torah itself says we should deal kindly with the Egyptians, one generation after we leave their land. The obvious question is: how can G-d justify the plagues?

The answer, I believe, starts with Yosef (Joseph).

In this week's Torah reading, Yosef buys the land from the people. As the verses state:

"So, Yosef bought all the land of Egypt for Pharaoh; for the Egyptians sold every man his field, because the famine was sore upon them; and the land became Pharaoh's. And as for the people, he removed them city by city, from one end of the border of Egypt even to the other end thereof... Then Yosef said unto the people: 'Behold, I have bought you this day and your land for Pharaoh. Lo, here is seed for you, and ye shall sow the land... And it shall come to pass at the ingatherings, that ye shall give a fifth unto Pharaoh, and four parts shall be your own, for seed of the field, and for your food, and for them of your households, and for food for your little ones.' And they said: 'Thou hast saved our lives. Let us find favor in the sight of my lord, and we will be Pharaoh's bondmen.' And Joseph made it a statute concerning the land of Egypt unto this day, that Pharaoh should have the fifth; only the land of the priests alone became not Pharaoh's." (Gen 47:20-26)

I tried to imagine what this displacement would have done to those displaced. They were divorced from their lands. They were separated from what they had known. Then, they were resettled. They were rationalized. The experience may well have destroyed them. The dream of the cows is a dream of the emaciation of the nation – not its food, but its spirit. In the process of making the Egyptians into shells of people, Yosef also made Pharaoh into the most powerful man who ever lived; the perfect foil for G-d in the story of the Exodus.

To bring this to life, I chose a modern corollary. All over the world there are native people displaced. In many cases they are displaced by higher economic uses for their lands, dams among them. Once they are displaced, they cannot go back. Their societies are often ripped apart by the social pressure of being unmoored from the basis of their existence.

Of course, given the opportunity they will want to capture what they feel is due to them: the productiveness they were displaced to allow. The dam in the story provides great economic power as do oil facilities in Nigeria or mines in South America. The Children of Israel are seen the same way in Egypt. Yosef was responsible for the disruption in Egyptian life. Because of this, later generations feel they should be able to harness the power of the Jewish people. They enslave the Children of Israel, hoping for material gain.

When they fail to realize their goals, they try to destroy the Children of Israel just as the people in the story promise to destroy the dam. When the plagues come, like the army of the government, the Egyptians are simply shells of people who have chosen to enslave and then destroy others.

They are first cut adrift by their own decisions and then they are condemned by them.

Yosef started the process in this Torah reading.

I don't believe Yosef meant to do what he did. He worked hard; I believe he worked to save lives from famine. But his decisions undermined Egypt just as they undermined his own family. We read:

"And Joseph sustained his father, and his brethren, and all his father's household, with bread, according to the want of their little ones." (Gen 47:12)

By paying them welfare, 'by the want of their little ones', he took from them the opportunity to dedicate the product of their hands to the sustenance of their own children. While we must support the poor who cannot earn a living, extending this to those who need not be poor takes from them one of the most basic ways we can dedicate our creative effort to the timeless relationship with G-d. It takes from them the ability to support their own future. It creates people fundamentally in the now, not the future. They lose a fundamental connection to the timeless that no ritual can replace. They lose true agency; they not only multiply, but the land fills itself with them (vatimale); and they teem (shirtzu) like insects (Ex 1:7).

However well-meaning his use of power, Yosef actually destroys those he is trying to help.

He keeps his family separate – but he enslaves Egypt and Israel alike.

It is a lesson in the limits of wisdom.

In the story, I wrote about spirits of the land and river and seasons. The Egyptians certainly believed the Nile had its own character. But the Chumash has space for a seemingly similar belief, although it is limited to the land. In later verses we see:

> For all these abominations have the men of the
> land done, that were before you, and the land is
> defiled-- That the land vomit not you out also,
> when ye defile it, as it vomited out the nation that
> was before you. (Lev 18:27-28)

> Then shall the land be paid her sabbaths, as long
> as it lieth desolate, and ye are in your enemies'
> land; even then shall the land rest, and repay her
> sabbaths. (Lev 26:34)

In these verses, the land has both rights and agency.

But its relationship to us and G-d is different than the relationship in the story. In the story, the people relate to the Most High through the spirits of the world. Many modern earth-focused belief systems do the same, relating to some fundamental life force through nature. But the Jewish people invert this; we relate to the Land through our relationship with the Most High.

While we must treat the Land with respect and while we must honor the limits of our own role in nature, we are forbidden from worshiping high places or seemingly powerful trees.

Everything must go through Hashem.

Although the relationship to the Land is valuable, it has no place outside of the relationship to G-d.

The people in the story (and perhaps the Egyptians) wove what they believed were the spirits of the river and the land into themselves. But we believe that we can weave Hashem Himself into our souls, directly. We believe this is open to all of humanity. We believe – I believe – this is a far higher and more fulfilling ideal.

Of course, it is also far more robust. Those who connect to Hashem can spiritually flourish even when surrounded by the supposed emptiness of modern life.

They can imbue the world around them with the spirit of Hashem.

p.s. the story borrows very loosely from the belief system of the Philippine Dumagats while the boiled cactus is borrowed from the South American San Pedro Cactus.

Vayechi: Time

I open my eyes and am greeted by the image of a woman. I think I know her from somewhere, she seems very familiar. I'm in a bathroom, and she is there as well. The edges of my vision seem hazy, the lights near the mirror seem ill-defined. But she is there. She's sharply defined.

She's sitting on the edge of the tub. Do we have a tub? She's wearing a half smile that seems unconnected to the darkness in her eyes.

She's looking through me.

I know her. I know her.

"Where am I?" I ask myself, confused. And then I remember the real question, "When am I?"

It has been this way for as long as I remember. I've been pulled through time, closing my eyes – even just to blink – in one time and then opening them in another. It seems to have gotten more frequent, though. It seems to have accelerated. I want desperately to return to the present, but I can't seem to find *when* it is.

"Beth?" I ask, not entirely certain. The woman is so beautiful, she could be Beth, couldn't she?

The woman on the edge of the tub looks up. "Jacob," she says, her voice flat. It is a voice somewhere beyond bitterness, like all the anger and resentment has been spent and there is no more to give.

I've been here before, in this place.

No, in this time.

"Beth," I say, "What are you doing?"

She reaches to her side, and I see it then. A small box. A plastic box. She has medication? I watch her open the box, slowly and deliberately. And I realize that I've been here before. But I can't remember what happens next. It, like the lights near the mirrors, is just beyond my understanding.

I watch Beth opens the box. There's a syringe there. It has a twister on the side, so different dosages can be provided. I see her take a needle from the box and place it on the top of the syringe. And then I see her twist and twist the selector, choosing the maximum possible dose.

And then I know what is in the needle.

Insulin.

And I know what is about to happen. She pushes the needle into her own arm and she places her finger over the depressor. I lurch forward to stop her. I can't allow her to kill herself. I have to stop it.

And then I blink. And I'm someplace else.

Some *time* else.

And I know I've failed.

The world comes into focus again. A hospital room this time. This is more familiar. A child is about to be born. I see the mother, a woman whose face is pale with the challenge of labor. She's sweating and angry and worn-out. A doctor is there. "PUSH" the doctor says. And the woman bears down, her whole body seeming to tense in determination. And then, seemingly moments later, there is a child. A baby.

Whose baby?

I look at the child – a boy – and I see he is beautiful. The doctor shows him to me, smiling. And then she brings the baby to her mother. The woman. Beth? But the mother, Beth, looks away. She does not want to see this child. Something is wrong with this child.

But he looks so beautiful to me.

I step towards the doctor. I step towards the baby. He is new to this world. He needs reassurance. He needs love. And I, at least, have love to give. I take the baby in my arms. I blink back a tear of joy.

And then, I am gone.

Now I know when I am. The man in front of me is my brother. We're at our parents. There's a party. A party for him. Why?

I see people milling around me. Some are familiar. But I'm just a child. I'm maybe ten. My brother is much older. He's in his twenties.

I feel like an unwanted extra.

Did he graduate from college? Win a game? Does he play football?

He's standing next to something. A box of some sort. It is tall, taller than he is. He calls the crowd and they come. Gathering nearby. My parents are there. Scientists. They are *all* scientists.

They gather closer. There's electricity in the air. A buzz. An excitement.

My brother has created something.

Then, as the tension seems to crescendo, he pulls open the doors on the cupboard. The little crowd surges forward. Somehow, I'm at the front of them. I look up at the now open box. It has a glass front with small holes perforating it. And inside? Inside there is a person. He looks like my brother. Exactly like my brother. But he is just standing there, locked in the box.

And then the person – is it a person? – opens its eyes. And I see them, and I know they are empty.

The man in the box has no soul. I feel myself turning. And then running. I'm fleeing between the feet of the scientists as they ooh and aah at my brother's masterpiece.

And I remember what it is.

It is a clone, with no brain.

"No higher mental function."

That's what they called it.

He, it, is spare parts.

I'm in the garden now. I'm angry, sad, revolted. Tears flood my eyes for reasons I can't understand. They don't help. They can't help. And then, in a moment, I know what can.

I blink away the tears.

And then, again, I am gone.

When I open my eyes, I'm standing on a freeway onramp. I look down at my clothes and realize they are old and unwashed. I smell terrible. I'm holding a sign, begging for money. When am I?

I reach into my pocket and find a wallet. It has almost nothing in it. But it has an ID, my ID. The young man in the photo is maybe 20 years old. How did I get here? I look at my sign, expecting it to ask for money. But instead, it says "FIGHT CRISPR?"

CRISPR? Is it a misspelling?

No, it isn't a misspelling.

As I think about it, the word fills me with anger. I know I must fight CRISPR. But I have no idea what it is.

Then I feel something, in my other pocket. I reach in and I pull out a flyer. "FIGHT CRISPR" it says in bold lettering. Then as subtitle, "Humanity must have boundaries."

Then, I understand. CRISPR is "Clustered Regularly Interspaced Short Palindromic Repeats." It is a tool for editing genomes, including the human genome. It was what my brother used to create his spare parts. It is why I am on a street corner. I've been fighting CRISPR.

I've been driven from my parents' house, and I've been driven from every job I've tried to hold.

I've been fighting CRISPR. But CRISPR has been destroying me.

The traffic rolls off the freeway, coming to a stop at the light. Most people leave their windows up. But some take the time to rolls their windows down. To give me the finger or spit in my direction. In the back of these cars are children. They all look beautiful. Unflawed. Perfect. I can tell their ages by their appearances. Their coloring and features follow the fads, fashion statements and social trends that dominated the years of their births.

"Editors," I realize, "Everybody has become a gene editor."

And *I* have achieved nothing but my own suffering.

I see a marker pen sticking out of the side of the small backpack at my feet.

I turn over my sign and scrawl out, "ANYTHING WILL HELP."

And then, as the traffic rolls away, I hold up the new message.

A minute later, it comes to a stop again. No one rolls down their windows to spit. But one window does roll down. A hand reaches out, with money. I step towards it.

I look in the window. There is a woman there. She too is beautiful. But something is different. And then I see it. It is a flaw. Her mouth is pulled up on one side, unwillingly. She turns away from me as I look.

She is ashamed of herself.

But she is the most beautiful woman I have ever seen.

I blink, and all of it is gone.

Now, I am in a darkened room. It is huge and almost empty. I don't remember this place.

Am I back in the present?

There's a man in front of me, and a child.

The man is my son. I know that. I look at him, admiring him. He seems beautiful and perfect. But I know he is cursed. How? I cannot remember *how* he is cursed.

"You must keep fighting," I say to the young man. "You have inherited my mission."

He nods.

I blink.

And then I am pulled back again, and out of the present world.

I open my eyes in a clinic. There are soft colors all around. She's there. The beautiful woman from the freeway offramp.

Beth.

But she's angry now.

Something is wrong.

I look down at my hand. I'm holding a report. A genetics report.

Stamped at the top is ***FETAL AGE: 6 WEEKS***.

I scan it quickly. There are two sections: "Susceptibility" and "Possibility". Low intelligence, low-fitness, a range of diseases – all are marked "Low Susceptibility." On the other side of the ledger, possibilities abound. Only one item breaks the trend. Diabetes. Our son's susceptibility is high.

I see Beth's face again, screwed up in rage.

"*I TOLD YOU!*" she shouts at me as the clinicians look on.

And I know what she told me.

She told me to design this fetus. She told me not to let nature take its course.

She screams, "HE WILL BE CURSED!"

But she is not talking about the diabetes. She is talking about the increased risk of Bell's Palsy. She is talking about her own 'imperfection.' She is speaking of her own flawed humanity.

But she is not flawed.

Even as she shouts, I smile at the paper before me.

"Am I G-d?" I ask.

She looks at me, uncomprehending.

She doesn't understand. She can't understand that I do not know what perfection is.

Perhaps the child's perfection will be what *we* think of as a flaw.

With that thought burrowing through my mind, I close my eyes in joy.

When I open them, I am back in the massive and empty room. I am in the present day. I can feel it. Time is unfolding slowly before me. Like it used to, long ago.

And the man and the child have returned. I know the man. He is my son. My imperfect son.

He is beautiful. I look at him like I haven't seen him in years. Perhaps, in a way, I haven't.

And there is a child there as well. But I do not know him.

As I watch, the boy comes close to me. He looks at me, staring into my eyes. He has such powerful eyes. I feel myself reaching out to touch his face.

And then, once again, I leave the present. But instead of being thrown back into the past, the future rushes towards me. He is my grandchild. I see his future and that of his children and his children's children. His future is dark indeed. But then in an instant I understand that *I* can change it. And so, I do. I see attempts to hijack my legacy, but I blunt them. I see weakness and anger, but I moderate them. I see those who lack of self-control, but I reinforce them. I see leadership with the risk of perversion, but I straighten it. I see those who would knit the people together and I strengthen them. I see those who embrace law and I reward them. And then I see a surge forward, my descendants' attack on a world edited beyond understanding. And I rejoice in it, satisfied and encircled by the beauty of their long-awaited victories.

I open my eyes and I see the child. My grandson.

I smile at him, happily.

And then I close my eyes and I am no more.

The Grandson's Story

I must have been five years old when I saw my grandfather die.

My father had raised me to always look forward and never back. He'd raised me to always learn from regrets and mistakes, but not to dwell on them. He taught me to focus on a mission greater than my own life or my own talents and weaknesses, whatever that mission might be.

He taught me all of this. I had it all in mind as I entered the ward, and I looked up at its sole resident.

My grandfather.

My grandfather was sitting in a wheelchair. His eyes were open. But he was mumbling incoherently. I drew close and I heard him speaking of Beth – my grandmother. I heard him speaking of her death. Of their union. Of their child. And I listened to the ravings of a man who was no longer truly there.

I was filled with loss. I can't remember ever being filled with such tremendous suffering. Such tremendous regret. It almost overpowered me. I was filled with the suffering he no longer even knew existed.

And then I thought that perhaps the others were right.

After all, my grandfather was alone on the ward. All who would have been otherwise here were euthanized. Some voluntarily, some volunteered by others. Perhaps my grandfather should have been among them. Perhaps it was better that we no longer locked up those who were slowly melting away.

But my grandfather would not accept the alternatives. He embraced imperfection. He insisted on it.

His life was an imposition and a criticism of the world.

He loved to argue that killing those who suffer was not the same as eliminating suffering.

Except *I* was suffering, and my father was suffering. And, perhaps, my grandfather was not.

I drew closer to the old man; I don't know why. Perhaps I wanted to embrace him, to place my own will over my resentment.

But then he reached out and he touched me.

In that moment, his eyes opened wide. And he began to speak about the future.

He began to speak of *my* future.

I watched him, somehow held in the palm of his hand.

I listened.

I learned.

And I found myself overwhelmed by his wisdom, the wisdom of a demented old man.

Then his hand withdrew, he smiled at me, and I watched him close his eyes for the last time.

Yosef grows to be a man who motivates others by instilling them with purpose. Pharaoh follows him because Yosef tells him that he can rescue the land. He pours himself into his purpose; travelling constantly to carry out his own mission. He focuses so clearly on his purpose that he is willing to overlook the past to create a better future. He seems to marry the daughter of his old master; the master who had him jailed. He is willing to walk away from his own family and their competitive struggles. When his brothers show up, he does not kill them or deny them food, he builds up their character and the leadership of his brother Yehuda.

Finally, he feeds and cares for his brothers' families – even after the death of their father.

I believe Yosef and his wife Asnat raised their children with those same values.

As Rabbi Sachs points out, Ephraim and Menashe are the first two children in the Torah who do not fight. When Yaacov is blessing them and their primacy is switched and then switched back, neither complains nor struggles with the other. They have their eyes not on competition, but on the greater picture. They are looking to their shared purpose in the world.

When we come to the opening of Parshat Vayechi, we see Yaacov as an old man mentally weakened by his age. He drifts between the present and the past. He seems to relive his wife's burial. Then he is overjoyed at seeing his son, as if he had not seen him since he disappeared. But he does not recognize his grandsons.

It all changes when he touches his grandchildren. It is almost as if their focus on the future pulls him into that future. In a Torah consumed with the idea of converting the physical into the timeless, this is one of the most tangible examples.

A member of my community described wisdom as the perspective of the experienced. Yaacov's wisdom is fragmented. But when touches two children who are living in the future, because of their dedication to purpose, he enters the realm of prophecy.

At the end of Bereshit (Genesis), the Torah shows us a man brought low by age. It does not do this to embarrass Yaacov. It does it to educate us. The weakness of Yaacov does not diminish what we can learn from him.

Perhaps, just maybe, the opposite is true.

Our weakness may just hold the key to our power.

As Yaacov shows us, we can change the world until the moment we draw our last breath.

Author's Note

The Biblical Joseph was given *useful* interpretations when he gave credit to Hashem for his understanding. He finally gave full credit to G-d when he said:

בלעדי: אלקים יענה

"It is not in me, G-d will answer."

I am not a scholar. Instead, I often finding myself asking Hashem for an answer to difficult questions. Almost invariably, a little while later, I find the answer I need, and it becomes a part of what I share and what I write.

I don't think this is anything unusual. I believe *all of us* can do this. We just have to be open to asking, and then be ready to listen to the answers we are given.

Joseph Cox lives in Modiin, Israel and is blessed with a wonderful wife and six children. If this book added to your life, do someone else a favor and share it. Also, *please please* add a review online. It makes an enormous difference.

That's me!

Other Books by the Author

Adult Fiction

The City on the Heights (a novel)

Candidate Everyone

The Hidden Agent

The Boulevard, Torah Shorts Volume 2

The Assessors, Torah Shorts Volume 3

Pete and the Felon, Torah Shorts Volume 4

The Barn, Torah Shorts Volume 5

Children's Fiction

Grobar and the Mind Control Potion

Squiggles and the Pit of Destruction